LOST WORDS

LOST WORDS

Nicola Gardini

Translated from the Italian by Michael F. Moore

A NEW DIRECTIONS PAPERBOOK ORIGINAL

Published by arrangement with Marco Vigevani & Associati Agenzia Letteraria.
Originally published in 2012 as *Le parole perdute di Amelia Lynd*

This translation was made possible by a grant from the Zerilli-Marimò Prize/City of Rome for Italian Fiction. The writer and translator also gratefully acknowledge the hospitality of Writers Omi at Ledig House.

First published as New Directions Paperbook 1338 in 2016
Manufactured in the United States of America
New Directions Books are printed on acid-free paper
Design by Erik Rieselbach

Library of Congress Cataloging-in-Publication Data
Names: Gardini, Nicola, author. | Moore, Michael, translator.
Title: Lost words / by Nicola Gardini ; translated by Michael F. Moore.
Other titles: Parole perdute di Amelia Lynd. English
Description: First New Directions paperbook edition. | New York : New Directions Publishing Corporation, 2015. | "Originally published in 2012 [Milano : Feltrinelli] as Le parole perdute di Amelia Lynd" —Verso title page.
Identifiers: LCCN 2015038045 | ISBN 9780811224765 (alk. paper)
Subjects: LCSH: Working class—Fiction. | Teenage boys—Fiction. | Older women—Fiction. | Mentoring—Fiction. | Milan (Italy)—Fiction. | GSAFD: Bildungsromans.
Classification: LCC PQ4867.A7225 P37113 2016 | DDC 853/.914—dc23
LC record available at http://lccn.loc.gov/2015038045

10 9 8 7 6 5 4 3 2 1

New Directions Books are published for James Laughlin
by New Directions Publishing Corporation
80 Eighth Avenue, New York 10011

In memory of my friend, Idolina Landolfi

Odd that living in anger should be so pleasant! It involves a kind of heroism. If the object against which one railed yesterday should die, one would immediately set about looking for another. "What shall I complain about today? Whom shall I despise? Could that person be the monster? . . . Oh joy! I've found him. Come, friends, let's tear him to pieces!"

SILVIO PELLICO

. . . and use words taken from dictionaries, as remote as possible from common speech.

MARIO VARGAS LLOSA

I

The telephone woke me up with a start.

"Who's calling at this hour?" my mother grumbled.

I set my feet on the floor and went looking for my slippers. Once again my father had kicked them toward the fridge as he walked by. Then I flipped my cot back inside its cabinet. With her mouth hanging open and one hand on her forehead, my mother listened to the voice on the other end of the line. The clean-up bucket was still on the doorstep, half in, half out.

I made it to the window just in time to catch two policemen hopping into the squad car and taking off to the home for the severely disabled. It was another gray fall day, and the cat, lying in the middle of the courtyard, was wiping her paw over her face, as she did whenever there was a threat of rain. A patch of fog floated over from the pile of rubble across the street.

"How am I going to deal with the tenants now?" my mother said as she hung up. "I need this like I need a hole in the head . . ."

She started mopping the lobby, going at the marble floor with enough energy to carve grooves into it. When she came back inside to change the water, I couldn't keep my mouth shut a minute longer.

"Mom, it's September 21 today . . ."

"Oh sweetheart, forgive me," she chirped. "Of course it's September 21. Thirteen years ago, at this very hour, you came into the world, my little bundle of joy! Happy Birthday, honey! Your father wanted to wish you a happy birthday, too, but I told him to let you sleep in today."

She fumbled around in the pocket of her smock and pulled out a crumpled piece of ash-colored paper. A one-thousand-lira note.

"Here," she said firmly, in a voice that stressed her magnanimity.

And it was indeed a magnanimous gesture, but I barely got a peek at the thousand-lira banknote. Like her presents on birthdays past, the money was quickly deposited in the toolbox, to which she alone had the key.

"Now be a good boy and drink your milk—there's the bread. Dip it in the milk if it's too stale."

By early afternoon even the tenants at 15 Via Icaro knew that during the night burglars had broken into two apartments in the building next door. The victims were still away on vacation—the Biaginis and Signor Quarone, the contractor. In the lobby shrieking clusters of women gathered, fretting that their homes would be next. There was no escape. Once the robbers had you in their sights, it was only a matter of time . . .

I observed them through the glass door: they kept engaging and interrupting each other, giving each other impatient little shoves as if they were fighting. The truth was that they were terrified. I had never seen them like this. Because this time it was a question of money.

"We can't tolerate this violence!" thundered Signora Dell'Uomo, indignantly. "Burglary is rape!"

Although embarrassed by the comparison, Signorina Terzoli nodded her agreement. Signora Mellone, never at a loss for words, repeated to anyone who would listen: "At Signor Quarone's they went through every closet and every drawer. Then they fried themselves up some eggs as if they had all the time in the world. They even left a banana peel on the kitchen table!"

Dell'Uomo acted stunned, even irritated, that she hadn't been the first to ferret out every detail. Not a woman to be outdone, she came up with her own version of the facts: "Well I heard it was a crust of bread," and added, "besides, who told them to stay away on vacation till the end of September anyways?"

"If they break into my place, they won't find a damn thing . . ." Signora Vezzali boasted. "I don't keep checks or cash in my house. I always keep my money with me, right here." She patted the secret pocket sewn into the inside of her skirt. "If they want my money, they're going to have to take me first—and that would make it kidnapping . . . do you think it'd still be worth it for them?"

"Not for all the money in the world," my mother muttered between her teeth, standing a few feet away. "What would they want with an old bat like you?"

Signora Zarchi, ever irreverent, laughed her head off at all the drama. She wasn't afraid of thieves: "There's no such thing as thieves! In the end we're all thieves, aren't we?"

"Speak for yourself, Signora Zarchi," was Dell'Uomo's swift rebuke. "I've never taken anything from anyone. My conscience is clean, I don't know about yours . . ."

She and Vezzali traded malicious looks.

"Ladies, ladies . . ." my mother tried to calm them down. "Ladies!" But her pleas were useless. They, the *signore*, were too worked up to hear her, too intent on playing the victim. They ignored her with unvarnished contempt, as if she, the doorwoman, were immune to such dangers by virtue of her occupation: to put it bluntly, a doorwoman, by definition, was not a *signora*. But was that enough to make them signore? Hardly. On Via Icaro no one had ever laid their eyes on a real signora. Respectable people kept their distance. Well, there were always a few exceptions, of course. Men, by and large. According to my mother, men were a hundred times better than women. Not always, of course, but often.

"Take someone like Pasquale Petillo, that nice tall bachelor: as good as gold, and he never gives anyone any trouble. Naturally Dell'Uomo can't stand him. She says she's seen him bringing black women home. So what—who cares? Aren't black women just the same as other women? What a shame he decided to move back home to Calabria ... God help us!"

Word was already out that another *signora* would be moving in to take over Signor Petillo's apartment, a woman who lived alone ... Maybe she'd be an old maid like Terzoli or the younger Mantegazza ... she had a surname that was either American or German: Lynd. Now mind you, it's Lynd with a "y," as the building manager had emphasized when, in an unusual phone call, she'd announced the arrival of a "fine, upstanding" person.

"But of course," my mother had quipped, "all the fine, upstanding people are dying to make Via Icaro their home address!"

They demanded *around-the-clock* surveillance. The doorwoman was not to be away from her post or distracted for a single instant. If something required her to be away from her post, like taking out the trash, then her son should fill in for her and guard the lobby and the front staircase. After nine o'clock at night, the front door had to be double-checked to make sure it was actually locked (sometimes the humidity made the lock stick). And the gate had to be equipped with a spring mechanism (some careless people were in the habit of leaving it open) . . . Oh, and we also had to make sure that the large windows between floors were closed and that their chains were tightly latched. Mellone and some of the other women actually expected us to start announcing their husbands' arrivals.

"Poor me," my mother complained. "The last thing we needed was for everyone to be worried about burglars! When is that damn landlord going to make up his mind to sell 15 Icaro? . . . Take a deep breath, Elvira. Just hold on a little while longer and you'll be an owner, too. Oh, Chino—can you imagine? I won't have to say Good Morning and Good Evening to anyone! Once I close my door, it'll stay closed. I won't have to worry about another living creature!"

My father came home from work and wished me a Happy Birthday in his own way, by predicting how old I would be the coming year.

"Next time around you'll be fourteen, and that means no more fooling around. By the time my cousin was fourteen he was already a father himself!"

He didn't have a present for me. He didn't give a damn about birthdays, not even his own. Mom was the same. She only cared about mine because it reminded her of the day she became a mother. Holidays and anniversaries didn't mean anything to her. She thought they were a waste of money. You had to know how to manage your money, setting it aside and only using it when necessary ...

She told him about the burglars, forcing herself to act more upset than she really was.

"I can't take it anymore. I want my own home!"

"What's that got to do with burglars?" he objected, already sunken deep into his armchair and scanning the front page of the evening tabloid.

"It's got everything to do with it!" she replied. "I'm fed up with always having to follow orders ... there's always some new problem. Once it was the pervert jerking off by the front gate, or the time Mantegazza left the gas on, or when Terzoli mistook a giant rat for a cat and was about to start petting it. Then there's the Jehovah's Witnesses sneaking up the stairs ... and the Avon ladies, who are even worse than the Jehovah's Witnesses ... And now burglars! Each and every time—no matter what happens—the first thing the tenants do is ask for Elvira, *Elvira come here, Elvira go there* ... Don't you get it? The burglars aren't the issue. The issue is this job. I'm sick of it. It's time for me to have my own home."

"What do you think this is? Isn't this a home?" He said without looking up from his paper. "Here we don't have to pay rent or electricity or phone bills. Where are you going to find another place like this? Who's got it better than us?"

"I'd rather pay for my own gas and electricity, thank you. This is no way to live."

"You have to learn to tell people to fuck off! But no, you're always bowing and scraping. You've got to stop saying yes all the time! You're a disgrace to the working class. You need to act more like me!"

"And you're such a fine example? ... *Good evening, Signora Paolini!*
... It's easy for you to talk, going out early in the morning and not
coming back till late! But I've got them staring over my shoulders
all day long. They even look at what I'm eating! I choke on my food
when I have to say hello to them. I don't have enough time to go to
the bathroom ... or to finish my sentences, like now. Don't you see?"

She started setting the table.

"In the next few months," she continued, before my father could
change the subject, "if I work hard, I should be able to save up another million liras! Dell'Uomo's relative has promised to pay me fifty
thousand for the wool blanket I'm crocheting for her. And there's
plenty of ironing and sewing to make some extra money ... *Good
evening, Signor Vignola.*"

Rather than continue on his way, Vignola slid the window open
and poked his head in.

"It'll only take a second, Elvira. I just wanted you to remind my
upstairs neighbor that in the apartment you're supposed to wear slippers, not leather shoes. The sound of his shoes is driving me crazy!
And tell him that if he doesn't have enough money to buy a pair of
slippers, then I'll buy them for him!"

"Of course," my mother agreed. "When I see Signor Malfitano
I'll let him know."

"No, I'd rather you called him right away!" he demanded. "And if
that *asshole* doesn't knock it off, tell him I'm going to call the cops."

My father gave the intruder a look but didn't intervene.

"Do you see what I have to put up with?" my mother complained
after Vignola had left. "The neighbor's bothering him so I have to be
the messenger! Unbelievable! These good-for-nothings want to rob
me of everything, even the air I breathe."

My father tried to ignore her, but couldn't: "I'm not going to
throw away my hard-earned money on those crooks selling houses.

Have you taken a good look at the prices? You've only got two options: either sign up for public housing or go on strike. That's what we do in the factory when we don't like something. It's not that we expect to become the boss or anything. But you don't understand—first you want an apartment, and God knows what you're going to want next. If it were up to you, every day you'd be shopping downtown at the big department stores. You can't change where you came from. When you're born a doorwoman, you stay a doorwoman. Can't you get that through your head?"

"What are you talking about? I wasn't born a doorwoman and I'm not going to stay one. And you don't say 'doorwoman.' The proper term is 'custodian.' 'Doorwoman' makes me sound like a streetwalker. A custodian is a caretaker, and that's is exactly what I do."

"What a bunch of bullshit!"

"This isn't only about us. It's also about Chino. What kind of a life is it for him, sleeping in the loge. You can hear everything: the front door slamming, the elevator going up and down, the voices of people coming and going, the refrigerator ... It's never really dark, so he wakes up tired—don't you, Chino? It's a sacrifice for you, too, sweetheart!"

My father didn't see the problem. When he was a boy he barely slept. At two in the morning he'd go out on his bike and deliver bread while bombs were dropping all around.

"There you go again!" my mother cried. "When you don't know what to say, you always bring up the war ... I can't even remember the war."

I'd heard it a million times before.

"I'm off," I said, although we still hadn't eaten.

My mother's instructions followed in my wake. "Don't forget to check that the doors to the balconies are locked. And make sure the chains are pulled. And stop by the Malfitanos'. Tell them politely that Vignola has been complaining. *Politely*, ok?"

I went up to the fifth floor and started checking off the things on my list. The neon lights were working. No one had left empty bottles by the trash chute. The balcony doors were locked ... I saved Malfitano for last. He was surprised to see me. My face turning red, I reported Signor Vignola's complaints.

He did not keep me waiting for a reply: "If Signor Vignola has something to say, he can tell me himself."

Although summer had just ended, the temperature dropped suddenly and the signore started complaining that it was too cold. They'd forgotten all about the burglars. Now they were demanding that the doorwoman turn on the heat.

"Old hens," my mother used to call them. "You know what hens do when you toss them a crust of bread? They run to grab it. But if you toss another crust before they've finished the first, they drop it and go running for the second one. And if you toss them a third piece then they do the same thing again. You could cover them in pieces of bread and they'll always start pecking at the last one."

She explained to the signore that she couldn't turn on the heat. It was too early in the season.

"This is just the beginning of October. We need authorization. Do you want us to get fined by the city? A little patience, ladies. We'll light the furnace this year like we do every other year ... but please be patient. A little draft isn't going to kill you."

The only one who didn't complain about the cold was Bortolon. She had no intention of spending money on fuel—all she needed to stay warm, she was proud to boast, was her husband. Didn't the rest of them have husbands? ... In the meantime, she would light the oven—which was cheaper anyway—and bake a nice cake.

To console myself from all the hen-pecking, I started to fantasize about the person who was supposed to move into the Petillo's one-bedroom apartment, the woman with a "y" in her surname. Would she be different? Would she show more consideration for my mother? Or would she be just one more person tormenting her with stupid requests? Despite my mother's forebodings—all based on experience—I imagined Miss Lynd to be kind and respectful, even if I still couldn't picture her face or her voice ... For me her essence was summarized in that strange surname, Lynd. Lynd, Lynd, Lynd— shimmers of music, tinkling of silver ... All the others were coarse and ugly by comparison: Dell'Uomo, Bortolon, Mellone, Terzoli, Paolini, Mantegazza ...

"Momma, when is Signor Petillo moving out?" I asked impatiently.

"What's it to you?" she replied, surprised I would care. "Sooner or later he'll leave, don't worry. He's waiting for his transfer to come through ..."

Having been bombarded with complaints, the building manager ordered the heating to be turned on earlier than usual this year. It had been authorized by the municipality.

"Fine," my mother conceded. "We'll turn it on. The signore want heat? They can have it. Let the whole bunch of them burn alive!"

The maintenance man came to check the furnace. He cleaned out the tank and the first fuel shipment was delivered. We turned it on and the water started boiling in the pipes, spreading warmth through the apartments. What a blessing! No more shivering. The laundry dried in a second. The older Mantegazza stopped coughing. You could lounge around the apartment in a T-shirt—even without socks, even bare-boot, since the marble floors were no longer ice-cold ...

After dinner my father took me to the boiler room, down a steep and narrow iron staircase outside the building. In all these years I'd never been there before—it wasn't a place for children.

"This is disgusting!" he complained while unlocking the gate. "That damn cat comes down here to pee ..."

In the basement's dim light, we could make out a small furry shape that recoiled and leapt behind the straw broom, sheltered from the autumn wind.

We went down the last flight of stairs, covered with ugly gray tiles. There the temperature rose because the burner was near and it was noisy. My father stood fearlessly in front of the bulky furnace. Swift and efficient, he showed me a black lever, next to the main thermostat, which was easy to make out against the body of the burner.

"Like this ..."

All you had to do was turn it. In that very second, the sound of the flames quieted down. Now it was a whisper, a voice that had lost its terrible power.

A decision had been made: from now on turning off the furnace would be added to the list of my evening chores. I was thirteen, after all.

"HE DOES IT ON PURPOSE! HE DRAGS HIS FEET! AND
THEN HIS WIFE, WITH HER DAMN HIGH HEELS, ADDS
INSULT TO INJURY!"

Vignola's voice over the intercom was so loud that my father and I
could hear it from across the table, ten feet away. My mother wrinkled her nose. She hadn't even finished chewing her food.

"Malfitano told me to tell you, Signor Vignola, that if you have
anything to say to him, you have to say it to his face. He doesn't want
to hear about it from me."

"AH! SO THAT'S WHAT HE WANTS! WELL THEN TELL
HIM, PLEASE, THAT IF HE FORCES ME TO GO UPSTAIRS
I DON'T KNOW WHAT MIGHT HAPPEN. THIS COULD
GET UGLY!"

"Calm down. Signor Vignola. These walls are made of paper."
And after giving me a complicit look, she pointed a finger at the
ceiling, indicating that we could hear both him and his wife peeing
in the toilet and even worse, fooling around in bed. "We learn to live
with each other ..."

Vignola was beside himself. In the background there was a high-
pitched chatter, the shrill voice of his wife egging him on.

My mother was having trouble swallowing her food.

"What a mess! We have to do something. Do you remember that
guy, here in Milan, who shot his neighbor because she used to vacuum all night?"

"If you ask me they can all go kill each other," my father cut her
off. "They're nothing but a bunch of Christian Democrats anyway!"

"What are you talking about? Don't you realize we're stuck in the middle of this? We can't pretend nothing is happening! Vignola is going crazy!"

"Shut up already, I'm trying to listen to the news."

The IRA had planted another bomb.

"Now *that's* what I call killing each other," my father commented with a crooked smile.

The intercom buzzed again.

"DO YOU HEAR THEM? DO YOU HEAR THEM?" Vignola shouted, "THEY'RE TRYING TO DRIVE ME CRAZY!"

"Yes, I can hear them," my mother admitted, almost in tears. "What are they doing? Are they moving furniture around?"

"DO SOMETHING RIGHT NOW OR I'M CALLING THE COPS!"

My father went out to lock the gate and change the trash bags. My mother put the dishes in the sink to soak. In a daze, she stared at an invisible horizon that blended into the powerful gush of the faucet. Then, while I was getting ready to go out for my usual evening chores, she told me:

"Chino, can you please stop by the Malfitanos' and tell them that the whole building is complaining."

I went up to the second floor. From the Malfitanos' apartment you could hear the sound of furniture being dragged across the floor and the scraping of metal. A shadow broke away from a corner of the landing and came toward me. For a second I thought I was going to scream. It was Vignola gnawing on his fists. He stared at me, his eyes popping out of his face, begging for help and vowing revenge. We both stood there listening. The noise was endless ... Fearing the feverish stare of Vignola more than the wrath of the Malfitanos, I rang the bell. The noise stopped immediately and the door opened. The first thing I saw was the parrot, perched on Malfitano's shoulder.

"*Our father who art in heaven . . .*" the bird recited.

Malfitano appeared to be disappointed. Obviously he was expecting to find Vignola at the door.

"*Our father who art in heaven . . .*"

His wife, in the background, was pushing a big checked sofa toward the back of the corridor and sweating profusely. "Who is it?"

"The doorwoman's son," he replied.

"*Our father who art in heaven . . .*" the parrot continued.

Malfitano stuck a finger in its beak and the bird started to chew on it. Then it focused on his right ear. It pecked at the inside of his auricle methodically, scrupulously cleaning the inside of his ear. The lady of the house, blue in the face from her efforts, collapsed onto the sofa. From what I could see in the doorway, the living room was in complete disarray: the chairs were upside down, the table out of place, the Magritte posters askew.

"Tell your mother we're done for the night," the woman gasped.

Convinced I had done my duty, I headed for the upper floors. Vignola was standing and waiting. From the balcony I could see that he had lit a cigarette and was smiling like an idiot, triumphant.

On the fifth floor I looked for the door to Petillo's apartment and stood there for a while, filled with a strange and wonderful sense of expectation.

A beam of light penetrated my closed eyelids—it forced them open and I could see an arm moving just above my head, wriggling its way through a hole in the glass. (Now that everyone had stopped worrying about them . . .) I got up, careful not to make any noise, and ran to the bedroom. My father and mother were still sleeping. The glowing clock-face said that it was one o'clock in the morning. I shook my parents. They both immediately noticed the stream of light bouncing between the floor and the ceiling. My father leapt to his feet and ran into the other room. My mother held me. "Quiet, hush," she whispered in my ear.

Without wasting a second, my father grabbed a ceramic vase and slammed it against the arm. A shout rang out and the flashlight fell to the ground. My mother rushed to the kitchen. He kept squeezing the vase, which hadn't even cracked, as if he wanted to strangle it. We heard someone running down the driveway. My mother rolled up the blinds and saw two men rushing through the gate, but she couldn't recognize them in the nighttime mist. A moment later you could hear the sound of a car taking the road through the fields.

For once, my father was not so sure of himself.

"What if they have a gun?"

My mother tried to calm him down, but she, too, was upset, and she, too, was afraid that the thieves would come back soon for their revenge. She pushed the armchair against the door, but it was only as tall as the doorknob, leaving the hole in the glass uncovered. She leaned the table-top against the window, leaving two legs sticking out. Then she put the coffee pot on the fire.

"What are you doing? Call Cavallo's husband on the intercom," Dad ordered her. "He's big. Call everyone before the burglars come back. Wake everyone up, for Christ's sake! Those guys will be back with reinforcements and all hell will break loose!"

"You're crazy! I'm not calling anyone. You want a revolution? Let's call the police, instead."

Dad didn't want to have anything to do with the police—the only thing they were good for, as far as he was concerned, was killing innocent bystanders.

"You'll see, first they'll beat me up then they'll throw you in jail."

After a long wait, during which the criminals had all the time in the world to take their revenge on us, a squad car finally arrived. First, the cops requisitioned the burglar's flashlight, which had rolled under the table and was stuck between the foot of a chair and the stove. One cop stayed outside to inspect the lock on the gate and reconstruct the movements of the thieves. The other, an older man, sat comfortably on my bed, and told my dad, in a mocking tone: "You're a brave man."

My Dad, standing by the window, shrugged his shoulders.

"What was I supposed to do? Welcome them in? Hand my son over to them?"

"You're lucky they ran away. One time there was a burglar who started shooting at a tenant who caught him in the act ... Play the hero and you'll end up with a bullet in the head!"

"Maybe they learned from you ..."

The policeman didn't take the bait—he gulped down his coffee.

Although my dad couldn't provide any information that would help identify the criminals—the dialect they spoke, the accent they used, or the clothes they wore—it was determined that they must have been gypsies.

"Well, what did they want from us?" Mom asked. "What were they looking for in a doorman's loge? We've got nothing worth stealing."

But she was thinking about the checkbook and the pocket change—my pocket change!—that she kept hidden in the toolbox.

"The usual things you find in any loge," the policeman explained laconically. "The keys to all the apartments."

Everyone's eyes turned toward the white wooden cabinet on the wall above my bed, next to the circuit breakers.

Before leaving, the policeman advised us to replace the window as soon as possible and also to reinforce the door.

"Will they be back?" Mom asked.

"What do you want me to say, signora? Let's hope not . . ."

To avoid a fight, my father withdrew to the bedroom.

"What an asshole," he repeated, "like all policemen."

We waited for daybreak in front of the glass door, staring into the hole. Between one coffee and another my parents decided not to tell anyone what had happened. The demands for protection would only increase—and what more could we do?

"We have to move away from here as soon as possible," was Mom's suggestion.

At seven Dad left for the factory as usual. One hour later, without taking her eyes off the door, Mom called the building manager and told her what had happened. Signora Aldrovanti made no comment. She didn't say she was worried or that she was sorry. Luckily the break-in had taken place at night, or the doorwoman would have had to put up with all kinds of criticism. But given the circumstances, no one could blame her for anything.

"I don't feel safe anymore, Signora Aldrovanti," she whined. "Our boy actually sleeps in the front room of the loge. He was the one who gave the alarm, imagine how much courage that took. Another couple of inches and the intruder's arm would have touched his face . . . The very thought makes me . . ."

Aldrovanti was not one to let herself be swayed by emotions. What did we expect? For her to hire a bodyguard? For someone else to do our job? ...

My mother allowed herself to say that she wanted the door and the window reinforced—it was the least they could do, just like the other doormen on Via Icaro already had. The manager said we were free to reinforce whatever we wanted, but under no circumstances would the building reimburse us. The glass would be covered by the insurance, but everything else would have to be paid for by the doorwoman. One final and very important matter: since it was being vacated, Petillo's apartment needed cleaning from top to bottom. Miss Lynd deserved to be welcomed with the utmost regard.

The glass was replaced that very afternoon; the carpenter came the next day. He took the measurements and promised to deliver— within ten days—two dark wooden accordion boards, one for the glass in the door, the other for the glass in the window. He also convinced my mother that the door had to be protected with two iron bars. The metalsmith also came immediately to install the four wall-braces that would support the iron bars (but the bars wouldn't be ready for at least two weeks)—the loge took on the appearance of a jail cell.

Now it was my father's turn to sleep on the fold-out bed. Call it sleep! He spent most of the night on his feet, in front of the glass door. He would pull back the curtains to look out at the deserted lobby. Then he would get back in bed. The main door would slam. He would stand up and start spying again. From the bedroom, my mother could see the light. "Paride, go back to bed!" she would say in a muffled voice. But he ignored her. Someone was standing still in front of the elevator. Who was it? Then he would call for her help. "Christ, Elvira, come and see! How am I supposed to know everyone? Who signed the contract, Mary Mother of God, me or you?"

My mother's gestures started to become maniacal, betraying a nervous haste that tore objects from her hands or led her to use excessive force. She had gotten clumsy and careless—she, of all people, who usually handled everything so easily and skillfully. Now whenever she served dinner she'd spill food on the table. If a meatball fell on the floor, she'd pick it up. But at the sight of the stained marble she'd go nuts. "Look! Look at this mess!" she'd yell, as if it were my fault. And before getting out a rag and scrub brush, she would slap me across the face without realizing it. She slammed doors, caught her dress on the chairs, tripped on invisible obstacles. Every day she broke something: a glass, a cup, an ashtray ... In the kitchen, while she was using the knife, she cut her fingers and, more often than not, while she was eating, she would bump against the iron braces, which stuck out of the walls like giant teeth (I called them "fangs"). Her arms were always covered with bruises.

The trash chute got blocked up. Someone, to spare themselves the effort of going downstairs to the trash room, shoved a box or a fruit crate into it. Lately this was happening a little too often.

"May whoever it is drop dead," Mom swore. "Stay here."

She got the broom and went upstairs to take a look. After a few minutes I recognized the sound of her heels, which came at me faster and faster from one landing to the next, *ta ta ta ta ta tatatatatatatatatatata*, like a summer rain, the first timid drops suddenly turning into a cloudburst. Tapping from below with the broomstick, she managed to remove the blockage stuck halfway up the trash chute.

When she came back from the trash room, I almost fainted—a

wounded phantom appeared before me. The smell of blood forced me to turn away and close my eyes. Along with the blockage, a glass bottle had come down. I was sure my mother would bleed to death. She washed herself, removed a glass shard with her eyebrow tweezers, and I helped her bandage up her wrists. Then she asked me to wipe up the red spots that had dripped on the floor—which ran from the door to the windows to the bathroom sink.

My father returned from work, and since the blood kept seeping through the gauze, he accompanied her to the emergency room. I stayed behind to stand guard.

Signorina Terzoli came by to ask for a pint of milk. She always needed something. My mother was right to say that some people mistook the loge for a deli.

"My mother's not here," I said boldly. "She had to go to the hospital. Someone threw a bottle down the chute."

"Oh my goodness! ... Who's going to clean the landings now?"

I didn't give her a drop of milk. I told her we were all out. The old crone looked me up and down with irritation, and for a second I was afraid she was going to search our fridge.

"Listen, Chino," she went on to say with a sweeter tone, "is it true that Miss Lynd is a relative of Liz Taylor? That's what they say ... What do you know about the lady? Have you met her?"

I was unable to satisfy her curiosity. And even if I could've, I wouldn't have said a thing to her.

The sight of Elvira bandaged up to her elbows unleashed a thousand exclamations from the signore. For once they expressed some pity, but only because they shuddered at the thought of a shard of glass getting stuck in their own flesh. My mother, who thought any one of them might be the culprit, sighed: "I don't know who did this to me, but I wouldn't want to be in her shoes right now!" They ignored her all the same. They had already lost interest, distracted by the rumor that Petillo would be moving out soon and certain Miss Lynd would be taking his place. No one knew where she was from. Some suggested that she was arriving straight from Paris. Others ventured that she was Australian. Vezzali claimed that she had been the wife of an ambassador, but the others believed she had been married five or six times, like Liz Taylor—who she supposedly resembled—and had lived off her husband, until he lost all his money gambling or on younger mistresses. Terzoli kept insisting that she was related to Liz Taylor.

My mother cursed them, each and every one, because in her condition she could no longer work, like ironing for the signore in the buildings next door, or crocheting a blanket for Dell'Uomo's relative. The accident was going to cost her dearly. "You, my dear lady, owe me X amount for all the hours I was forced to sit around idly …" She would take her frustrations out on me, as if she were speaking directly with one of the signore: "And you, what do you think? You have to reimburse me, my dears! Do you take me for a fool? Well you're dead wrong. If I can't buy a house for myself on your account, then I'll kill you with my bare hands—I swear I will!"

One night, on his way back from the auto repair shop, Riccardo, the Lojacono's son, stopped by our loge.

"I heard about the accident, Signora Elvira. I'm so sorry."

Mother never imagined that the boy, who had been such a rascal when he was little, could ever have spoken to her that way, and with gratitude, she told him that he had become a fine young man, that holding down a job was good for him. Riccardo blushed, because the compliment had come from a woman who was still quite pretty, but also because, in all probability (the suspicion came to me immediately), he considered them undeserved. He, too, by coincidence, had a bandage on his wrist. To break free from my mother's insistent stare, he explained that a few days earlier a steel pipe had fallen on his arm ... Only a sap like my mother would've believed it. After he left she exclaimed, "What beautiful blue eyes."

Signora Aldrovanti refused to pay for damages: my mother had gotten hurt, but it was her own fault—she knew there were certain risks in the trash room, she should've been more careful, the way a good doorwoman is expected to be. You have to pay for your mistakes. Next time she should wear safety gloves. "And if next time the glass ends up in my eyes?" mother protested to me. "What am I supposed to do? Put on a ski mask before I enter the trash room?"

To prevent more accidents, I made five signs, one for each floor of the building, which I taped to the balcony doors.

IT IS PROHIBITED TO THROW GLASS
BOTTLES DOWN THE TRASH CHUTE

Now my father had to do the chores before leaving for the factory. He got up at five, raked the leaves in the courtyard, mopped the landings, dusted the main entrance, and polished the elevator panels and the mailboxes. During the day the trash bags were replaced by the neighboring doorwoman, from Via Icaro 18, whom mother had promised to compensate with a wool sweater as soon as her wounds were healed. She kept watch—the only thing she could still do—with her forearms resting on the table.

Idleness was making her even more irritable. She was constantly yelling at me: "Stand still!" "Don't touch!" "Shup up!" Or, if another little boy was within range, she would start picking on him for getting mud on the hall carpet or yelling at him for not saying hello when he passed by on his way home from school. She would follow him up the stairs like a woman possessed, raising her bandaged wrists. "Hey, you!" she would shout. "What did I tell you?" The child would stutter, "Excuse me," not knowing what he was being accused of. Ignoring his apologies, she would make a scene that always culminated in an attack on the upbringing he'd received from his parents: "Go ahead and tell them. I've got a piece of my mind for them, too!"

Hoping to lift her spirits, Dad thought it would be a good idea to invite a colleague to lunch the next Sunday. He explained that the guest was Tavazzi, a union organizer, who, like all union organizers, had sold out to the bosses. Not to mention that he was an opera lover, a *loggionista*. But for now, given what had just happened to him, they had to turn a blind eye. Two of his three children had been hit by a car on their way to school, dying instantly. The only one left was the youngest, who was more or less the same age as me.

My mother was happy to invite the poor things over, especially since we had no friends apart from the two neighboring doorwomen, who every now and then dropped by for a cup of coffee.

On Sundays the loge was closed. Even if we were having a grieving family over, we could still pretend it was a holiday. Despite the curtains pulled over the door and window, the iron braces in the wall, the fuse box and the intercom, we could still act like we were living in a normal house, like everyone else. My mother, cursing the bandages on her wrists, cooked enough for an army.

If we hadn't been aware of the tragedy, we wouldn't have noticed anything amiss about our guests. When mother said, "Condolences," according to the ritual she had been taught since childhood, they reacted as if it were the dumbest thing they had ever heard. We looked like the ones who were in mourning.

They ate heartily. Signora Tavazzi was not particularly friendly—she seemed more shy than suffering, even a little surly, in the unique manner of certain southern Italian women (she was, in fact, from

Puglia—she reminded me of one of the tenants, originally from Molfetta, Signora Perotta, who had lived on Via Icaro for only a short time but stood out for her haughty peasant airs). She didn't even ask mother why her wrists were bandaged, a fact that couldn't have escaped her. So Mom volunteered the information, though obviously minimizing the gravity of her injuries—the accident was nothing compared to losing two children simultaneously. Signora Tavazzi, having heard the explanation, remained emotionless.

Signor Tavazzi, on the other hand, was cheerful and light-hearted. He treated Dad like an old friend, and Dad played along with it. He was also friendly to Mom and me. In moments of silence he whistled. He spoke to us about Russia—what a strange place! People lining up everywhere, and total silence, even in the subways. Not to mention the prohibitions: don't go there, stop here ... it was all you could do to keep from breaking the rules. The streetcars were operated by women. And everywhere they sold ice cream, even in that polar cold. And the Moscow subway—it reeked! But the Bolshoi was gorgeous. And only the best of the best went to school. And the chambermaids at the hotels, they could be had for the price of a Bic pen. And you could only buy caviar at stores for foreigners. Oh, and another good thing to buy was amber.

"Filomena," he said to his wife, "show them the necklace I brought you back from Moscow."

With two fingers, she lifted up a string of pink beads from her chest. Mother exclaimed: "Oh, so that's what amber is! I thought it was plastic ... Filomena, did you go to Russia, too?"

"No, not me ..." Pointing to the child sitting next to her, she added, "but he went ..."

The boy didn't bat an eye, as if he hadn't even been mentioned. He had a nasty look on his face. We didn't talk at all. He even avoided my gaze. But I was so fascinated by what I knew that I couldn't take my eyes off of him—although I'd never met them, I could see the faces of his two dead brothers in his stare.

Once the long lunch ended, Dad and Signor Tavazzi went out. Dad had convinced him to go to the movies.

The women started clearing the plates. To break the silence, Mom told Signora Tavazzi, who was passing her the dirty dishes and glasses, that we would soon be moving: the landlord was selling and we were going to buy the Vignolas' one-bedroom apartment upstairs. The woman, as mechanical as a robot, listened without a trace of curiosity. She said that she and her husband had no intention of buying. They were fine with low-income housing. Some months they didn't even have to pay rent, since no one would come by to protest. And then, even if they did come by, who cared about the municipality! ... She wouldn't say a word about the dead children. Not a word, even in passing.

"What a tragedy," Mom said, to draw her out, unable to restrain herself any longer. "I'm so sorry—did they at least arrest the driver?"

Signora Tavazzi ignored her. Mom found nothing more to say and took a few deep breaths while she dried the dishes.

"The Lord giveth and the Lord taketh away," the woman said out of the blue, "and we gotta learn to accept everything He sends us."

Mantegazza threw the grocery bags under the fuse box and flopped down on a chair. It took her a few minutes to catch her breath. She rummaged through her patent-leather purse, lit a cigarette, and after inhaling a puff of smoke, started to speak.

"Elvira, you're never gonna believe what happened to me today!" She hissed the words, as if a band were playing in the pit of her stomach. "At three in the afternoon, who should arrive, without warning, but the Tax Inspectors! Thank God they wasted time in the Manager's Office. I rounded up those four southern bumpkins that work off the books. I threw some of our customers' furs at 'em and told 'em to scram for a couple hours. You shoulda seen how happy the real fur coat made 'em! Would you believe they left by the front door, still wearing their work clogs, and those idiot officers didn't even notice 'em? Thank God! Then I scrammed, too . . ."

"You?!" mother was amazed. "Why would they go after you?"

"I'm retired and getting my pension, my dear Elvira." She started toying with the doily beneath the ceramic vase. "If they catch me still working—penalties to pay! I didn't know which way to run. For a second I even thought of diving in the swimming pool. Total desperation. But I hid inside a locker in the locker room. I thought I'd suffocate to death! And those guys took their sweet time. I almost started coughing. God, what torture! I was dying for a cigarette. Finally they left. 'Everything's in order,' they said. What an ordeal! When I stepped out of the locker I was more dead than alive. I told the manager, 'I'll be expecting a bonus at the end of the month.'"

Every now and then Mom would give me a look, as if to say, "Does she think we really care about all this baloney!"

Mantegazza seemed to catch her drift.

"Elvira, I'm worried about my mother. She spends too much time alone."

She opened her purse, took out her compact, checked her makeup.

"And you? Why do you keep working?" mother asked. "If I were you, I'd enjoy my money and call it a day . . ."

"And then what? Me, sitting around smoking all day? . . . Ma keeps telling me, 'Paola, it's time to retire . . . you need to rest . . .' She wants me to spend my time with her . . . She's lonely . . . Elvira, I was thinking. In the afternoons, around two, you could maybe go upstairs and keep her company? Only for a little while. You could chat, have a cup of coffee . . . "

Mother burst out laughing.

"Are you kidding? No way! I have to guard the door. I'd be in big trouble if I stepped away from my post! What kind of a *custodian* would that make me? . . . Not to mention the constant threat of burglars!"

The fat powdered cheeks of Mantegazza shook with disapproval— she hadn't expected no for an answer. She placed the compact back in her purse and started to roll back the edges of the doily.

"But I'd pay you!" she whispered conspiratorially.

"Maybe I could send Chino up," Mom proposed, after a very short pause for reflection, "He could do his homework while keeping Signora Armanda company . . ."

The sound of those words knocked the wind out of both Mantegazza and me. She even twisted her head around, as if someone had stuck a knife in her back.

"For heaven's sake!" she exclaimed, without making the least effort to hide her contempt. "My mother *detests* children! . . . Do you know what I think? My mother could come downstairs to you, here in the loge, and ..." Rather than finish her sentence, she removed a can of coffee from one of her shopping bags. "Just half an hour ... two or three times a week, after lunch ... All you have to do is call her on the intercom and say, 'Signora Armanda, come on downstairs. We can have a cup of coffee together.' As if it were the most natural thing in the world ..."

"But ..." Mom tried to object.

Whatever she was going to say remained stuck in her throat, because at that point Mantegazza opened her wallet and plucked out a nice pink banknote.

"Take it!" she ordered, looking away. "And don't go telling Signora Armanda I gave it to you, or she'll start screaming and yelling. You know how she is ... She's still pretty feisty. If she finds out I threw away money on this, there'll be hell to pay."

Mantegazza was right: her mother detested children. The first time she came into our apartment, in addition to the disgusted look she gave me, she kicked me in the shins, striking me with the tip of her foot while I was helping her to sit down. My jaw dropped, more from shock than from pain. What had I ever done to her? I barely knew her!

"Come, come, Signora Armanda," my mother soothed her, "sit there, that's good, in the corner ... There you won't bother anyone. Now no one will find anything to say ... In the meantime I'll put a nice pot of coffee on the stove ... Chino, come here and twist on the top of the coffee maker. I've got no strength left in my hands ... How are you? Did your cough finally go away?"

The old woman emitted a long sigh. She was wracked with pain, she said. Everything hurt: her legs, her shoulders, her head. She couldn't go to the bathroom, couldn't sleep, her diabetes was getting worse ... And now she couldn't digest anything. All she could eat for lunch was a small plate of pasta, a grilled beefsteak, and an apple. Mom raised her eyebrows as if to say, "Well, then. You certainly won't die from starvation." She nodded at me and I went into the bedroom.

I pulled the curtains aside and looked out the window. The sun had become colorless and no longer hurt the eyes. It stood still in the middle of the sky, hovering over the desolation of Via Icaro like a worn-out coin. The leaves were shriveled on the cement of the courtyard: swept by the wind, they would swirl about, stop, and start racing again as if they had a will of their own. The branches on the sycamore trees had whittled down to a few naked stubs. Only the rows of thorn bushes remained unchanged, as red now as in summer, like blood against the pale white of the air and the grounds. Without the foliage, whose shadows created tremulous wandering shapes during the fair months, the courtyard looked bigger, as gray as the sky looming over it from every side. No one played out there this time of year. Only Rita continued to come down despite the cold. I could see her jumping up and down to keep warm, speaking to someone, either aliens or the cat, holding a bunch of yellow leaves.

Signora Mantegazza's voice carried all the way to the bedroom—she was defending the Milanese dialect: "Who speaks it anymore? Only old people like me. The younger generations might understand it—but can they speak it? Forget about it. The only ones who speak dialect in Milan anymore are those southern bumpkins. They speak their *own* dialect, which is garbage. Arabic. They've taken over the city. *Animals . . . Abyssinians!*"

Southerners, to her, were all thieves, liars, and lazy bums. All the post offices were run by them. Who knows why—and they were always on sick leave! Poor Milan! Everything had changed! Even during the war Milan had been beautiful. And then there was Him. A god! In 1937 they had their picture taken together. It seemed impossible that there had ever been a *man* like him, who filled you with strength and hope. And order!

"Long live the Duce! Long live the Duce!" she shouted in a frenzy.

She tried to stand but fell back down in the chair like a sack of potatoes, huffing and puffing. Mom patted her hand and rearranged the clump of hair on the nape of her neck, reinserting the comb that had fallen on the floor. The old woman's face was aflame, flushed by the renewed surge of energy, but her body, unequal to her passion, shook with empty tremors. All the while she kept grumbling that nowadays the world was going to hell in a hand basket. No one

wanted to work. Young people were a disgrace! They all belonged
in reform school, maybe there they'd learn some manners. Or better
yet, to war with them—no better school than that! We needed another war. Without war no one learned anything. You didn't know
whether it was the parents' fault or the teachers'. Back in her day—
ah, those were the days—if you didn't do what you were told, you
got a good kick in the pants. But today's parents and teachers were
always explaining how and why to children. What is the world coming to? Children are supposed to obey orders without demanding
explanations!

"Chino!" my mother called. "Go outside. You need to rake the
leaves, sweetheart ..."

Rita said it was fun to rake. We were in front of the fountain with the gold fish, where the remaining dry leaves had crumbled to dust. "Would you like to be a fish?" she asked.

"Of course," I replied, because right then I hated everything—the leaves, the cold, and especially nasty old Mantegazza.

I stared enviously at the motionless school of fish, gaudy against the green muck on the bottom of the pool.

"Not me," said Rita, "I'd want to be a bird, because birds live in the sky, like astronauts."

Pietro and Matteo came by. They told us they had just been to the home of the disabled to steal cookies from the spastics.

"If you don't believe us, look," said Pietro.

Both boys opened their jacket pockets wide to show us the loot.

"What the hell are you two doing?" asked Matteo, kicking at the rake and the bag.

"Nothing," said Rita, "we were playing rake the leaves . . ."

"I know a better game!" suggested Pietro with a malicious smile. "You ask me a question and I answer. If I don't tell the truth, I have to pay a penalty."

"Fun!" Rita exclaimed.

"Yes, lots of fun," Matteo confirmed.

He told us the rules: for every wrong answer, you had to remove one piece of clothing. The first one to be bare-chested was the loser.

Rita, the fool, said it was okay with her. She was already laughing at the thought of seeing the two of them with their teeth chattering from the cold.

I said I didn't want to play, hoping that would convince them to drop the idea and leave us alone.

"Who asked you, anyway?" Matteo sneered.

We went behind the building, where no one ever went and hardly anyone looked out the window.

"Rita," Matteo began, "answer the question, true or false. Do I like pussy?"

"True!" she said with a hand over her mouth.

"Are you stupid or what?" Matteo shouted at her. "What makes you think I would like that stinky hole you've got between your legs? Wrong. Take off your coat ..."

Rita quietly obeyed.

Pietro didn't want to be outdone by his friend.

"In your opinion ... is it true or false ... true or false ... that ... you'd like to take it in your mouth?"

"Take what?"

Pietro squeezed his crotch.

"My banana!"

Flailing her arms, Rita shouted, "False! False! No, no!"

"Wrong!" Pietro decided. "You're dying to suck it. To suck both of us ..."

Rita shook her curls with a dismayed expression that filled me with anguish.

"No, it's not true, I swear it's not ..." she tried to defend herself.

"Never tell a lie!" Matteo interrupted, "or you'll end up in hell. Better to take it in your mouth than to tell a lie ..."

"Exactly," Pietro confirmed. "Now take off your sweater!"

The other boy repeated the order.

I mustered up my courage and tried to stop them: "Stop torturing her ..."

Pietro shook his fist under my nose.

"Well look at that ... the little doorboy has spoken!"

He took the plastic sack, turned it upside down, and scattered all the leaves we had raked.

"If you don't like the game," Matteo added, "then scram. No one asked you to stay."

Pietro petted the peach fuzz that was starting to grow on his upper lip.

"I think he has a nice little pussy between his legs, too ... That's why he doesn't want to play ..."

Matteo burst out laughing and Rita copied him.

"You do, don't you!" Pietro pressed on.

He tried to strike my testicles with the back of his hand. I managed to dodge him and I retreated a few feet away. Rita was shivering from the cold. Pietro kept teasing her.

"What nice little tits!"

Matteo reached out to grab her. She shielded herself and asked them to stop, but they jumped on top of her. I tried to get between them but Pietro—who was stronger than me—shoved me aside. Although she was thrashing and screaming like an animal, they managed to take her pants off, too. Then Matteo, from behind, pulled off her T-shirt.

"Give me back my clothes," Rita shouted. "Chino, help me!"

Matteo dared me, "Go get them, if you can ..."

He rolled her clothes into a ball and threw them as high as he could up into the skeletal branches of the magnolia tree.

Rita didn't know what to do. She covered her breasts with her arms while Matteo squeezed her around the waist, restraining her and egging on his buddy, who fondled her however he pleased, just to humiliate her, without showing any display of pleasure. She begged them to stop with a tiny voice.

"Leave me alone! Please!"

While I was struggling to recover her clothes, climbing from branch to branch, the two boys were dragging her away.

By the time I reached them, Matteo was already bending Rita over the fountain. A few locks of her hair—which had come loose from her headband—floated in the water like algae above the dormant fish. But she resisted with a passive energy that would have been unimaginable only a few minutes earlier, while pressing her hands against the edge of the pool.

"Pietro, goddammit, help me out here!" Matteo shouted.

I grabbed him by his belt and tried unsuccessfully to pull him away.

Pietro, who at that point was standing back enjoying the show with his arms crossed, came over and punched Rita's neck. Her feet slipped on the gravel and in a second she sank into the fountain, head, torso, legs. From the look of surprise that humanized their features for a brief moment, not even her assailants had expected her to fall all the way into the water. The second she resurfaced, blue and dazed, they fled as fast as they could, as if a sea monster were emerging from the pool.

"I'm cold . . ." she sobbed, "I'm cold . . ."

I handed her clothes back to her.

To keep my mother from seeing her, I made her crawl past the window on all fours. Luckily the lobby was deserted. I withdrew to the bedroom and started counting. How long would it take Signora Zarchi to call on the intercom?

Mantegazza still hadn't left. She was energetically singing *Giovinezza giovinezza* while cradling a portrait of Mussolini. Once she had finished the fascist anthem, she started up with a Milanese folk song. My mother sang along with her, in a broken imitation of the local dialect. "What does the song mean?" she asked.

"Eh," Mantegazza replied, "the southerners are always going on and on about how great Naples is. But look at them here, lazy good-for-nothings, stealing our jobs."

The intercom rang, interrupting the song.

The priest opened the door. Without uttering a word, he accompanied me to the kitchen, where Signora Zarchi and her daughter were waiting. Against all my expectations, Signora Zarchi welcomed me with a benevolent smile. She didn't seem at all angry or threatening. Her clothes—quite colorful, as usual—conveyed an air of cheerfulness. She wore a purple tunic and around her neck she had tied an orange silk kerchief. Her blond hair was gathered behind her neck and held in place by a rose-shaped pin. An assortment of strangely-shaped brooches, crosses, long necklaces, giant rings, jingling bracelets, and anklets adorned every part of her body. Her feet were bare and her toenails were painted black, as were her fingernails.

Rita was sitting with a cup of hot milk, neatly dressed, and happy as a clam, in front of a wall-sized poster of snow-capped mountains—she could not have looked more different from her mother.

The priest opened a cupboard door, as if he were in his own home, took out a bottle of Johnny Walker, and poured himself a glass. Signora Zarchi invited me to have a seat. Then she withdrew to a corner of the kitchen. Padre Aldo suddenly raised his bald head and glared at me with two accusatory eyes. I quickly told him I had nothing to do with it—he should be talking to the other two boys. They were the ones to blame ...

"I'll take care of them later," he interrupted. "For now I want to speak with you. You were there, right? When Matteo and Pietro threw Rita into the fountain ..."

"Yes."

"So why didn't you do anything to stop them?"

I explained that I had gone to retrieve her clothes from the magnolia tree. I begged Rita to back me up, to tell him that I didn't want to play their game and that I had defended her as best I could ... if I had done any more they would have beaten me up!

Padre Aldo silenced me with a solemn gesture of his hand, to the delight of Signora Zarchi, who was hanging on his every word. He tossed down a gulp of whiskey and resumed his inquisition.

"The only reason we called you here was for you to apologize to Rita. The good Lord knows everything, it is beyond our powers to understand how and why. What is clear is that an innocent creature has been the victim of injustice. I imagine you must feel deeply ashamed about what happened, whatever did, in fact, happen ..."

I repeated that I had climbed the tree to retrieve her clothes, but my explanation mattered little to the priest. He said I had allowed myself to be an accomplice to a deplorable act, which tarnished my name and the good name of my family.

"You should be ashamed of yourself!" thundered Padre Aldo, lifting his glass.

He came so close to my face that I inhaled the whiskey on his breath and, for a second, I saw myself reflected in his glaring eyes.

"Taking advantage of a defenseless creature! Flaunting your physical superiority! ... Like an animal! God gave us reason—it's our duty to use it, starting in childhood. There are no excuses! Violence is even worse when it is exercised over the weak, over a representative of the fair sex ... Don't you know that women are the most fragile creatures in the entire universe? All it takes is a single episode to ruin her ... Women are delicate flowers, the most delicate ..."

He cast a knowing glance at Rita's mother, who was observing him dreamily.

"Any attack on a woman is an attack on life. By offending little Rita in that manner, you have offended yourself, you have profaned the most beautiful gift that has been given to you—the gift of being here, of being on this earth, of breathing this air. By the act you committed, you have become unworthy of this gift. Come now, ask for forgiveness! And with sincerity, with total love, otherwise it doesn't count! Rita, good girl that she is, might even find it within herself to forgive you. But it is far more difficult to receive forgiveness from the Almighty, who can look into your heart and recognize a lie ..."

I could feel myself suffocating. I gave a supplicating gaze to Signora Zarchi: exhausted, drunker than the priest, I begged for forgiveness. The Signora emerged from her corner, as light as a butterfly. She grabbed the glass of whiskey from Padre Aldo's hand and took a sip.

"I forgive you," she said to me. And to him, sweetly, "Aldo, that's enough. It's obvious that Chino is sorry."

The priest ordered me to apologize directly to Rita. She was the offended one. But rather than offended, Rita seemed amused: for her the whole scene had been nothing more than another game. I bowed my head and told her I was sorry. She repeated the same formula her mother had used. "I forgive you." The tension immediately eased up. The priest smiled at Signora Zarchi and she smiled back. Rita smiled, too. I was the only one to maintain a grave look on my face, which Signora Zarchi tried to erase by offering me a nice cup of milk. I mumbled that I had to go home to finish my homework. Rita insisted I stay. She dragged me to her bedroom and showed me her new television. A gift from Padre Aldo. It was a Telefunken, she explained, the best brand, as light as a feather. Even she could lift it and carry it around the apartment. Sometimes she even took it with her into the bathroom.

My mother was beyond the forgiveness of God. While I was in Rita's bedroom watching the portable Telefunken, the priest was telling her everything. When was I going to get it through my thick skull that I, the custodian's son, had to behave better than everyone else? I had to set an example! Instead of acting the same as all the others!

She was still carrying on when father got home. He heard the reason why, and burst out laughing: "When we were kids do you know how many times we fell into the water? One kid even drowned ..."

"There's nothing to laugh about," she shouted. "I want you to get on the intercom and say a couple things to the fathers of those two juvenile delinquents. Our son shouldn't have to pay for their actions! I take it back—it's not right that *I* should have to pay!"

My father continued to downplay what had happened. To him it was just kid's stuff. She should forget about it. What did the parents have to do with it anyway?

"It's not kid's stuff, for crying out loud!" my mother retorted. "They'll say: 'Well, who is the doorwoman to talk? She doesn't even know how to raise her own son.' I can already hear them. I have a reputation to defend. And you, if you're a real husband, you should stand up for me!"

"You're crazy! You can stand up for yourself! Isn't that what the feminists always say? That you don't need us men? That we're useless?"

"Don't even start with politics—I'm talking about *me*!"

"Who do you think I'm talking about?"

"There you go again, changing the subject. I tell you I want to move away from this place and you always complain about real estate agents ..."

"Alright already ..." my father gave in before she could start up again about wanting a house.

He went to the intercom and called down the fathers of the two boys.

They came immediately and loudly explained that Signora Zarchi had already met with Pietro and Matteo and that the boys had apologized. The Zarchi business was over. Irritated by their tone, my father demanded that they go straight back to Zarchi and lay the full blame on their sons. Rovigo turned pale. Paolini shoved my father and told him to worry about his own son. In a minute all three were in the lobby fighting like dogs. The stairwell was quickly crowded with curious heads peering over the railings. Rovigo called my father an idiot. Paolini aped his frenzied gestures, and looked around for spectators. My father argued that it had nothing to do with me and shouted that Pietro and Matteo were juvenile delinquents who were only going to get worse. Today they torture a playmate, tomorrow they rob a store and kill innocent bystanders ... My mother stared at him with an air of approval and a clear desire to be avenged once and for all ... Paolini and Rovigo traded contemptuous looks and left my father in the lurch with a loud "Fuck You!" My father made as if to chase after them but mother stood in front of him, crying "For the love of Pete." My father tried to break away, shouting "Fascist pigs!" while she put her hand over his mouth and pushed him into the house, drenched in sweat.

"What did I tell you?" my father gasped. "They were even swearing at me. They made a fool of me! We should have dropped the whole matter ... Fuck! ... But you? No!"

"Calm down!" she repeated. "Calm down!"

But he didn't want to hear it. He locked himself in the bedroom and started punching the walls.

"This year, come Christmas, there's going to be three fewer people who leave tips, you wait and see," my mother sighed, ladling the soup into bowls.

My father noticed the sign before coming through the front door.

NO COFFEE DRINKING IN THE LOGE

"Bastards," said my mother as she removed it from his hands.

She tore it into little pieces and explained that Mantegazza had come downstairs to the loge a couple of times. Yes, she had offered her a cup of coffee. What was the harm in that?

She was lying. Now the old crone was coming downstairs every blessed day. She would stay for hours until the sun went down. Soon we no longer needed to ring her on the intercom. She came on her own, as certain as death and taxes, and she also brought along her dog, Bella, who would curl up under the table, drooling.

"She's a fascist!" my father was indignant. "Once I heard her in the service room singing *Faccetta nera!*"

Mother's patience ran out. "So what! There you go again, putting politics into everything! ... This is my house and I can invite who-ever I want to come in!"

My father gave her a look as if to say, "Talking with you is a waste of time."

Saturday, on her way back from vespers, Signorina Terzoli stopped by the loge. After an unusually cordial hello, she started talking about how the recent rains had damaged the roof of the church. Padre Aldo needed money to repair it and she and some other women from the neighborhood had taken it upon themselves to raise the necessary funds from the parishioners.

"God bless you," said my mother. "When you've got money, it's great to use it to help other people."

Terzoli, ever the good Christian, wondered, "And who doesn't have a few liras to spare, Elvira? As long as its donated with a pure heart. Being rich isn't a matter of quantity. It's the gesture that counts. Isn't a child's sacrifice of a piece of candy worth more than a rich man's gift of a jewel to his mistress?"

"I can barely make it to the end of the month," my mother quickly protested.

Terzoli gave her a condescending look. "It's simply a question of good will, Elvira. We human beings are capable of putting up with the most grievous situations. All you have to do is want it. I'm thinking of you, Elvira ... I'm thinking of how much your generosity must cost you!"

My mother defended herself. "I wouldn't put it that way. This is my job and I'm trying to do the best I can ..."

"Elvira, generosity is a good thing, but you shouldn't let other people take advantage of you ... Not even God himself would want that!"

"You're right! Let's hope that one day God rewards me for everything I'm doing ..." She inspected the scars on her wrists.

Signorina Terzoli changed color. Her honeyed voice turned sharp. "Let me get straight to the point: the residents do not approve of the fact that every day you receive Signora Mantegazza in the loge. If everyone were to stop by Elvira's for a cup of coffee, what would the loge turn into? It's also a question of security ..."

Mother suddenly realized the treachery of Terzoli and the women who had sent her. "Signora Armanda is a lonely old woman," she stated with a saccharine smile. "Can't we just humor her? It doesn't cost me anything, and I feel as if I were helping my own poor mother, who passed away so many years ago ..."

The wrinkle lines on Terzoli's forehead smoothed out.

"Good for you, Elvira! Please don't get me wrong. I was just passing on what I heard, but I know, it's empty gossip. Some people think we should live with security guards at the gate! For heaven's sake, things aren't that bad, are they? We have to trust our neighbors. Padre Aldo himself said it in his sermon this evening."

When Signora Bortolon the seamstress invited me up for a snack, we knew she was up to no good.

"She's the worst of the lot," my mother warned.

I had certainly not forgotten what Bortolon had done a few years earlier to the Rossanos, the family from Messina who lived next door. I can still see their lovely little girl, who was born with long locks of hair. "Our Lady's braids" is what the Sicilians used to call that blessing from God. They would all worship her. I can still hear the shrieks of her mother when her daughter came home one day after Signora Bortolon had invited her over for a treat. Her locks were gone! Not long after the mother died from that act of sacrilegious violence. The widower was forced to return to Messina with his orphaned little girl to live with an old aunt.

The seamstress welcomed me with open arms, making a big fuss over me. She was alone. Her daughter Rosi had gone to the zoo with her father, as she did every Sunday.

"Come in, come in, Chino, you handsome boy," she cooed, "I've made you some nice zeppoles."

Following the trail of fried food, we went into the kitchen, where, on the table, as sticky and greasy as a skillet, a tray of piping hot zeppoles was waiting for me.

"Eat, eat! Not even your mother makes zeppoles this good. Have you seen the nice hole in the middle? They're all for you. Eat, you handsome boy!"

I obeyed, knowing it was some kind of trap. I didn't have the "Our Lady's braids" on my head, in any case. What in the world did she have up her sleeve? . . . Death by poisoning?

The zeppoles were exquisite: aromatic, soft, dripping with oil that trickled onto my chin and fingers. For a napkin the seamstress handed me one of the many fabric remnants lying all over the kitchen floor. Everywhere you looked there were traces of her work, mixed in with household items: threads, scraps, pieces of tracing paper ... The rest of her apartment was a junkyard. The sink overflowed with trash. The floor was speckled with rotting vegetables.

The seamstress observed me with satisfaction and encouraged me to eat to my heart's content. She was sitting in her chair, near the window, next to a dress dummy whose torso was pierced with pins. Like us, in the winter she used as much natural light as possible.

"Handsome boy, do tell me," she asked with a feigned nonchalance, while measuring a length of thread. "Does old Mantegazza visit you every day?"

Almost against my will, I answered yes. A part of me wanted to punish the seamstress. Another part wanted to compensate her for the zeppoles. I hated her maliciousness, but in that moment I was grateful to her for having prepared me one of the best snacks I had ever eaten.

"And she stays for a few hours, right? ..."

"Yes."

"Does the old woman like coffee? Does your mother make it for her?"

"Yes."

"Does she have a cookie?"

"No ... all she has is coffee ..."

"And what does she talk about? ..."

"She talks about when she was young ... She was in love with Mussolini ..."

"She doesn't talk about her daughter?"

"No."

"What else does she talk about? Come on, you can tell me ..."

Sick of this line of questioning, I told her we couldn't stand old Mantegazza, that we would be happy to get rid of her, but unfortunately she kept coming downstairs. The seamstress's face lit up. She said if my Mom wanted to get rid of the old woman so much, she could. If she didn't, it meant that she was getting something out of it ... Yes, of course, I admitted after a brief reflection, while the seamstress held her breath, as alert as a cat watching a sparrow. "Yes, Mom is getting something out of it," I admitted, "but we have also lost our freedom ..." I wanted to see how far the seamstress's curiosity would take her. She let out an exclamation as if to say, "So I wasn't wrong after all!" And how much did she get for it? How much did my mother pocket? ... Chewing the last zeppole, I said Mantegazza had promised to leave all her worldly possessions to my mother.

"Everything!" she shrieked. "What does the old woman own? I can't believe it! The estate should go to the daughter ..."

"Millions and millions," I embellished, more and more amazed at the power of my words. "And a house on the Riviera. The daughter agrees ..."

"A house on the Riviera ..." she repeated.

She was flabbergasted by the news. She remained speechless, frozen in her chair, with the needle suspended in the air.

"But my mother isn't asking for anything," I added. "She doesn't want anything from anyone. The only thing she wants is a little freedom ..."

The conversation was coming to an end. I wiped my mouth and went back home triumphantly, certain that I had finally put her in her place.

My mother was crocheting, very slowly, since her wrists were still bothering her. I sat near her and told her the seamstress had asked me a lot of questions. She frowned. What kind of questions? What did she want to know? "She should be trying to keep her house clean rather than worrying about hiding money under the mattress!"

I told her that the seamstress wanted to know whether Mantegazza had given us any money. "I said that we've gotten something, but in exchange we've lost our freedom ..." I tried to embellish my account as much as possible, using words like "victim," "slavery," and "prison," so my mother would be overwhelmed with gratitude.

As soon as I finished my tidy little report, her whole expression changed. Her eyes narrowed into slits and her mouth hung open without uttering a sound. For a second I didn't know how to interpret her transformation, but it soon became clear—a scream erupted from her mouth and her fists rose in the air. Her work fell from her hands, the yarn was pulled, and the crocheting began to unravel, row by row, devoured by an invisible set of teeth. I had never seen her so enraged. She jumped to her feet and tripped over the blanket. Terrified I would have to pick up the mess, I ran to lock myself in the bathroom. She kept on screaming: Why did I have to go sticking my nose into things? By now the seamstress had told half the world the doorwoman was making money off the flesh of that old woman! And they already had it in for *doorwomen*! The last thing she needed was for them to start accusing her of being *a mercenary*! ...

I thought I had gotten the better of the seamstress, and instead she had gotten the better of me. All for a plate of zeppoles!

I was filled with loathing, an abyss opened beneath my feet. Amid my tears I wished death on the seamstress, on all the tenants ... I wanted to die, too. My mother was right, this was no life. I bent over the toilet and stuck two fingers down my throat. At least I wouldn't owe anything to the seamstress.

The seamstress appeared in the morning, as usual, a few minutes before eight, holding her daughter by the hand. Sensing the approaching danger, she quickened her step. My mother blocked her path.

"Signora Bortolon," she said, her voice emphasizing the "Signora." "Can I have a word with you? . . . What in the world were
you thinking? If you want to know my business, why don't you ask
me directly?"

The seamstress batted her eyes.

"I don't know what you're talking about . . . What'd I do?"

"You know very well . . . Let's not beat around the bush . . . *He*"—
she pointed to me—"is a witness. You gave him the third degree,
that's what you did! . . . But if you must know, I don't get one cent
from Signora Armanda, so you can wipe that thought from your
head."

The seamstress dropped her act.

"That's not what the boy told me."

My mother was not about to be bullied.

"He lied to you," she lied. "I don't get money from anyone. My
son was just playing games with you! How could you think I would
take money from that poor old woman! My family gets by with the
money we make—through our own hard work! Understood?"

Bortolon gave her a long, nasty, and skeptical look, as if to say, Do
you really expect me to believe you?

"And besides, the loge isn't supposed to be a café."

"No. In fact, it's my home. And I only let in the people I want."

"Not during working hours."

"Signora Bortolon, I think it's fair to say I have never neglected my duties. Am I wrong? You tell me, when have I done a bad job?"

And with that she began a long litany of services, renunciations, and sacrifices that I'd heard a thousand times before.

That same afternoon, at the last minute, Mantegazza called on the intercom and said she'd rather stay home, with Bella. She didn't feel too well, blame it on digestion.

The message couldn't be clearer: from now on she would be drinking her afternoon coffee with someone else.

II

C ome in, Signor Petillo. If there's anyone you can trust, it's me. Admit that you're going back down south to find a nice girl from your hometown," my mother teased him. "You men are always going on about us women, but in the end you can't live without us! Right? Well, better late than never ... I can see that a few white hairs have already sprouted on your temples. Of course, older men never lose their appeal ... It's we women who age too quickly ..."

By way of saying goodbye, he shook his head and handed her an envelope: "For all that you've done for me."

Two days later, Amelia Lynd finally arrived at Via Icaro 15.

For once the building manager wasn't exaggerating. Miss Lynd was no old hen, as my mother had feared. Not in the least. She was a noble, multicolored bird with wings to fly.

What made her distinct wasn't the clear signs of her superior breeding—apart from the two huge diamonds she wore on her left hand, as if to symbolize the excellence of her person, but without affect, without flaunting it—no, there was something superior about her, a light radiating from her skin. Her body was incredibly thin, her clothing a necessary if somewhat studied piece of fabric enveloping an almost immaterial physique. Without her diamonds, she was the embodiment of sobriety. No make-up, no embellishments. Her fine gray hair was combed back tightly against her scalp, revealing her high cheekbones and two small unadorned ears. The shape of her head reminded me of the bust of Nefertiti I had seen in my history book. How old was she? It was hard to say ... sixty-five, seventy ... maybe eighty? Her forehead was smooth and unwrinkled but she had the transparent, fragile skin of the elderly, and the back of her hands were flecked with dark marks of various sizes. Her features were delicate, aristocratic, refined by age.

The moment my father saw her, he nicknamed her "la Maestra"— the schoolmistress.

My mother, not only to honor her promise to the manager, but out of an instinctive sympathy, gave her a warm welcome and invited her to dinner with us. Miss Lynd thanked her with a broad smile, but it meant she was declining the offer. She smiled easily, laughed easily, and her eyes sparkled, affected by a slight strabismus. Yet she accepted, reluctantly, only a cup of consommé that I brought up to her. She ate with extreme moderation, she told me. In practice she lived on water alone, which took the form of tea or consommé. Sometimes, "out of gluttony," she allowed herself a glass of milk or shaddock—as she had been accustomed to calling grapefruit since childhood—or a piece of fruit. She spoke with a strange accent that was hard to identify. Her Italian was perfect but it did not sound like her native tongue.

My mother even offered to clean her two-room apartment a couple times a week and to take care of acquiring the few things on which the Maestra sustained herself. Only after a laborious negotiation did she accept the proposal, and they agreed on a fee, which mother would have gladly foregone. For her it was a privilege to help a woman like that, especially after having debased herself by serving someone like old Mantegazza.

The appearance of the Maestra sent the signore into a tizzy. All of their fantasies were overwrought at the sight of such a pure and elegant reality. Look at her posture! A real duchess! Did you see those diamonds? And hear her manner of speaking—so distinguished! You could tell she was educated. Yes, but not every aspect was in keeping

with the stature of such a personage. She dressed too simply, for example. "Obviously," Signora Dell'Uomo intoned, "she's a foreigner.
Foreign women don't care as much about fashion as we Italians. In
that field, let's face it, we're unbeatable. Mind you, her skimpy little
sweaters aren't made out of wool: they're pure cashmere!"

More than one of the signore tried to invite her over for coffee
or sought to ingratiate themselves through small acts of kindness,
hoping to learn a little bit about her life and get a peek inside her
apartment. But she proved immune to their flattery, not to suggest
that she was ever discourteous. To keep them at arm's length, all she
had to say, in English, was "No, thank you." Not even the seamstress
succeeded in gaining entry, though she was convinced she had won
her over with an offering of her famous bread pudding. Miss Lynd
uttered her kind refusal through an opening in the door. To the *no,
thank you*'s by which she became known, the Maestra enjoyed adding a bizarre allusion, a literary quotation, in English or Latin. So
in a very short time, one week at the most, she had been demoted
from the rank of duchess to that of oddball, and indeed a genuine
crackpot, who had something bizarre to say every time she opened
her mouth.

"For me she's the type that likes to have a sip . . ." Terzoli specu-
lated.

At my mother's demand I offered to help Miss Lynd unpack the last of her boxes. For once, she accepted without protest.

"*Thank you, my boy*," she said, "*thank you, indeed!* Otherwise, *chi sa*, who knows, how long they would have sat here unopened!"

Novels, poetry collections, dictionaries in different languages, colored-glass vases, ancient statuettes, and black-and-white photographs passed through my hands ... How could I not compare that refined private museum—which condensed a lifetime of travels and encounters—to the knick-knacks that occupied the shelf of my foldaway bed, the horrendous souvenirs that the signore brought back to us from their annual vacations? The Tirolese baby-doll, the old man with the pipe, the gondola music box, the little chest covered with seashells, the Sicilian wagon, the Sardinian nuraghe, the plastic Alpine star: an Italian menagerie that shook every time I got into bed.

The Maestra described to me the provenance of a small Lalique vase, the life of Flaubert or Cicero, the travels of Herodotus, *Bouvard et Pécuchet*, *Middlemarch*, *Anna Karenina* ... How the hours flew by! Never before had I spent such beautiful, wondrous afternoons ...

Of the various photographs in her possession, I was most taken by the portrait of a very serious bearded man. I asked if he was her husband. "Oh, no," she laughed, "that's Sigmund Freud!" She explained that Dr. Freud was the father of psychoanalysis, and that he had been her neighbor in London many years earlier. They used to have tea together and converse about any number of subjects, although he was gravely ill and had to struggle to form words.

"He disliked his own face. That's why you never saw him smile. But he had such an *interesting* face, don't you agree?"

Before going back downstairs, I was rewarded with a nice bowl of custard. She didn't even try a spoonful. It was an exquisite custard, saffron yellow, into which she'd crumbled a cinnamon stick with her bony fingers. I adored it. I adored *her*. Her every gesture, even the way she beat the milk and eggs and stirred the wooden spoon in the dented old pan, had something incomparable that transcended the act itself and elevated her above anyone I'd ever known. There was no one like her on any of the maps where I had lived my life till that day.

By the end of the week the Maestra's one-bedroom apartment was ready, but that didn't end my visits upstairs to see her. She wanted to have me there regularly for afternoon tea, she said. When I arrived, the kettle would already be on the stove, the smell of cookies filling the air. Sometimes I might even find the delicious custard again, steaming in the blue and white bowl from India.

At home I talked about her all the time, like someone in love: the Maestra knew everything, had read everything, had original opinions about everything ... "*Lies!*" is how she would rail against the false truths spread by "clerics," the generic term she used to indicate politicians, teachers, and priests. "*All lies!*"

She had her own ideas about the books Signorina Salma assigned us to read. The *Last Letters of Jacopo Ortis* was a patriotic manifesto, according to my teacher—but it was just the opposite for the Maestra. She saw it as an attack on false faiths, and thus one of the few Italian novels really worth the trouble of reading. Manzoni made her sick to her stomach. His *Adelchi*? Nonsense! *The Betrothed*? Bad, if not worse. But the sanctimonious prig was right about one thing: a dictionary was needed to create the Italians. Luckily he was not the one to write it. Otherwise can you imagine the definitions that might have come from the pen of a man who would dare to interpret the plague as a form of divine providence? The nineteenth-century Minister of Education who made *The Betrothed* required reading was a disgrace. The only part of the novel she would save was Renzo's vineyard ("a slip of the pen by an addled mind"), because it expressed a negative vision of human history and demonstrated a rare lexical competence.

When she learned that Silvio Pellico's *My Prisons* was on the reading list for my exams, she flew into a rage. "What a revolting book! ... It doesn't even mention imprisonment! ... All I can see in it is an account of daily sacrifices that concludes with a hymn to providence. Every page wallows in Catholicism! Unbelievable! Pellico had a grudge against Voltaire, the man who would have erased torturers from the face of the earth. And the style! Let's not even talk about the style! All those exclamation points! All those prayers! ... the writing of Luigi Settembrini is far superior!"

I didn't have the courage to tell her that, under the influence of Signorina Salma, I actually loved Pellico's book. But she and I loved it for different reasons: she for its patriotism, I because I identified with the author's suffering, which was so similar to my mother's. I loved the pages where Pellico wrote about how in his isolation he fraternized with the ants that appeared on his windowsill: like him, I had once fed sugar to ants on the windowsill of the loge.

Of all the books I had to read for my middle-school exams, the only one the Maestra liked was Verga's *The House by the Medlar Tree*. But that, too, she read in her own way. She couldn't have cared less about the family's misfortunes, over which Signorina Salma shed tears of compassion. No, Miss Lynd was looking for something else, the drama of language. "Poor Verga!" she would exclaim, as if she were grieving for an unfortunate friend. "I've never seen a writer who placed so much trust in his technique and so little in his words.

A *tragedy*, don't you think?" Among the Italians, her favorite authors
were the ones who plundered the dictionary, like Pascoli, Gadda,
or Landolfi. She also liked Leopardi immensely, for his powerful
brilliant criticism. Thanks to the Maestra I discovered his *Zibaldone*
and its pages on the garden of diseased plants. Out of love for her I
learned these passages by heart. Among the non-Italians her favorites were Flaubert and a few English writers—she often spoke of
Hazlitt, Stevenson, and Henry James. The masterpiece of English
prose, for her, was Doctor Johnson's introduction to his *Dictionary*.
Among the ancients, to whom she owed her education, her favorites
were the orators and the historians. She read and reread Herodotus
and Thucydides.

When I told her that in history class I was studying Italian unification she burst into laughter. "But my dear, there is no such thing!
... Let me explain, Chino. Now listen carefully." She took a deep
breath, searching for the right words. "The Italians never did unite!
Ci hanno provato—They tried but failed! And the signs of their failure
are everywhere. Can't you see them? The only people who talk about
unification are priests and fascists. If there really were an Italy, would
the Italians be so divisive, so egotistical, so deplorably vain? *Dov'è
il popolo*—Where is *il popolo*? The Italians have no idea what they're
doing! They have no idea where they're going!"

All she saw was a mass of individuals struggling and barely man-
aging to speak the same language. She saw a *population*, not a *popolo*.
Please, please, please!—let's not confuse the country with the state.
There never was a state. It's nothing but *fumo*—smoke and mirrors!
Back then some imbeciles went around waging war on the state,
planting bombs, but they didn't realize they were attacking a phantom. Instead there was a country. The country had a geographic
grandeur. With bombs you could only hope to destroy the soil
of Italy. She thought it was appropriate that Italy, the land of the

downtrodden, was shaped like a boot. The so-called Italians were the inhabitants of this spectacular boot, just like lice or other parasites that nest in discarded shoes in the attic. What I needed to understand—she stressed—was that Italy, unlike France or England, did not recognize a true connection between the political constitution and the people. The 1948 Constitution, in literary terms, was excellent. But the people? Awful! Why? Because the Constitution was a gift to them from a minority of thinkers who had fought against the war and against fascism. The Italians themselves didn't really earn it. The Italian Constitution was an ideal, something to hope for, but not something real. And this awful population would never live up to this ideal. They would only get worse. What kind of future could you expect when the fascist party still managed to be the fourth largest political party in 1972? What will the boot look like in twenty, thirty, forty years? Ah, she wouldn't be around to see. But I would. And what would I see? A mass of idiots, materialists, and *mangioni*—parasites! A freak show. Corruption would be rampant, fascism would come to dominate hearts and minds once again. People would forget how to think. Well, not everyone, and the few who were still capable of thinking would be forced to leave the country, or assimilate, if they wanted to get anywhere. Those who stayed would become cynical social-climbers, betraying their own intelligence. So let the school keep spinning its lies. One day I would get it.

And although I didn't understand everything she said, with all those English words scattered here and there, hearing the foreign sounds gave me an immense pleasure, even more than the already great pleasure of discovering such a different way of reasoning and understanding things. English made me feel refreshed, or rather uplifted, into the true dimension in which the Maestra had made me believe my life was destined to unfold.

I threw myself headlong into studying the vocabulary and rhetoric of Shakespeare's language, which was taught very badly at school, if at all. Every day I tried to memorize dozens and dozens of expressions, often repeating them to myself over and over, even in bed, reciting them with my prayers before falling asleep. After a while I started using them around the house, to answer my mother—who would look at me with perplexity and irritation—or to translate her responses into English. I began to punctuate my speech with expressions like "of course," "well," and "indeed."

At my request, tea with the Maestra became a language class: not without occasional digressions. She strove to correct not only my grammar and pronunciation but also my way of seeing the world. She would sit in the low armchair while I was at the table, in front of my India bowl filled with yellow custard. "Let's begin," she would say. And we would begin.

Much of the lesson was dedicated to learning vocabulary. The Maestra would look up words I didn't know in one of her many dictionaries and read me the definition. I quickly learned how to tell her in English what had happened that day at school, describing my teachers and classmates, or talking about my parents, the only people the Maestra never allowed herself to criticize. Nevertheless, by her very nature she represented a complete, radical critique of everything I had learned from them.

She often interrupted me to comment, to probe—without the least malice—to correct me, or to ask me for an explanation when I expressed myself poorly. If I didn't understand something, she would say, "Would you like me to repeat the question?" with delicacy and grace, savoring the honeyed tones of her own voice. And that honey blended like wildflowers in a spring meadow with all the adventures and encounters of her mysterious life, in an indefinable accent that was both foreign and familiar, and actually more than familiar, dripping from my ears down into my heart. And I prayed that the Maestra would continue to speak with me like that forever, while I jotted down in my notebook every detail of a life I hadn't lived, a life she was bequeathing to me through her words.

"What's your name?" she asked me one afternoon. I thought I had misunderstood the question. The Maestra already knew my name. But she insisted: "Do tell me your name. What is your name?" Although I was used to her unpredictability, I was completely confused.

"My name is Chino," I reminded her.

"Are you sure? Chino must be a nickname. I'd love to know your real name ..."

I had to admit that my real name was different. It was Luca. But no one ever called me that. Satisfied, she explained to me that Chino *literally* pulled you down. It meant "bent toward the ground." Chino— and to explain this she shifted to Italian—and it was the posture of a farmhand. Chino was the head of an old man who had received bad news ... "Go ahead, look it up in the dictionary ..." She preferred Luca. She said that, although the etymology was different, my name was similar to luck.

"Luca," she repeated, "The Son of Luck."

My mother didn't know what to say—only, with a somber air: "Go upstairs to see Riccardo. He needs you." For the first time I wasn't allowed to go to the Maestra. I conveyed the news to her over the intercom. "How disappointing," she sighed. "I'll see you tomorrow, then."

The Lojaconos' apartment was a corner unit with one bedroom. I knocked softly and right away they opened the door. It was the first time I had been inside. In the doorway I was greeted by three embroidered flowers enclosed in a frame, and a porcelain dish with the words, "Guests are like fish. After three days they stink," and a trout painted in the middle. The wall around the telephone was decorated with postcards. The air was stagnant with the smell of hot soup and damp laundry hanging to dry.

Signora Lojacano was perfectly still. She appeared wet and shriveled from head to toe, as if she had just emerged from a flood of tears. She had the face of someone with a bad cold. I noticed for the first time that she had two beautiful blue eyes, which she had passed on to her son Riccardo, but right now she looked more like his grandmother. "Go on in," she encouraged me.

I went down the hall and stopped at the door to his bedroom. Riccardo's voice invited me in. The room was sunken in darkness—the shutters were closed. I made my way to his big bed. "Can you see me?" he asked. I could barely make out his profile, his naked arms on the bed-sheets, the shape of his head against the pillow. His eyes and other facial features remained in the darkness. I lowered my gaze to the tassels of the satin bedcover, which were illuminated by the yellow light coming in from the hall, and I prayed to God to get me out of there as quickly as possible.

"Man did I ever take a beating," he muttered.

I could hear him fumbling with the light switch hanging next to the crucifix. Before turning it on he warned me, "Try not to get upset." He flicked the switch and in the cone of light you could see two half-closed eyes, all black-and-blue, a mouth covered with cuts, a broken nose ... He was unrecognizable. I couldn't even reconstruct his ruined features into a human face ... His lips were swollen into a weird smile. One of his front teeth was missing. His split upper lip was stained with fresh blood.

"They hit me everywhere, Chino. My head, my back ... it went on and on. At one point they even used a crowbar ..."

"Who did this to you?" I found the strength to ask. He started coughing and couldn't stop. "The fascists!" he said, in a strangled voice. "They nabbed me in Piazza Medaglie d'Oro, in broad daylight. They jumped in my car when I was stopped at a traffic light and pointed a gun at me. Where the fuck are the police when you need them? ... I felt like I was having a nightmare. We drove out of Milan. I don't know which road we took ... I was shitting my pants ... The only thing I remember is at one point, after I'd been driving for a while, we got off the highway and were in the open countryside ... We turned down a dirt road ..."

He stopped speaking. His eyes filled with tears and his upper lip shook, puffy and red. Slowly and with great difficulty, he pulled the covers off all the way down to his legs. His naked body was covered with marks from the beating. His right side was as black as coal, his upper body a patchwork of purple bruises. My eyes came to rest on his hairy crotch and I immediately looked away. But Riccardo wanted me to see.

"Take a good look," he insisted.

He lifted his scrotum. Some punches had even been landed down there. He pulled the sheet back up very slowly and started coughing again. His mother ran in with a glass of water. "Drink, drink ..." she said, lifting his head from the pillow. She sat next to him on the bed. "Are you ready for your medicine?" she asked him quietly. She patted his forehead and left us alone again. I stared at his face the way you might look at a lifeless object, an expressionless mask. Riccardo understood my repulsion. "You're shocked, huh? Don't worry. It'll go away ..."

Signora Lojacono came back holding a small brown bottle. "People are crazy, Chino," she explained. "Don't listen to anyone! Not a soul! Look at what they did to my son ... Now be a good boy and get along home to your mother."

"I spent my youth convinced that if I knew the exact meaning of words, it would unlock my understanding of things. I loved difficult words, obscure words, foreign words. Not neologisms, which aren't real. I had my own cult for dictionaries. Maybe all young people, whether they realize it or not, love dictionaries—I'd go so far as to say that children are the ideal lexicographers. They don't know the language of the community very well because they still think that meanings exist independently of people. You could write a fairy tale about it: Once upon a time there was a meaning ... *and then?* What happens to this meaning? ... Let's say it meets a little girl. And the little girl misunderstands it, that is to say, she believes it. A while later she discovers that the meaning doesn't only signify what it claims. One night she sees it in the company of a few adults and realizes that it behaves *in a questionable manner*—like a mother who says she's only your mother but later turns out to be the mother of many other children, and as a matter of fact, the meaning wasn't a meaning at all. It was a *word.* Meaning, by itself, doesn't exist! A word is a meaning that comes into contact with people and assumes a variety of appearances. Everyone sees a little of themselves in it, everyone understands what they can or what they want to understand. *Bello, ma ...!* A mother can be the mother of many children, even if each of them will say that she's his or her mother ... I know—it's a bad fairy tale ... One day I realized that I was the hero of this fairy tale. Yet there are people who have a lifelong belief in the absolutely perfect correspondence between words and meanings. *Lucky them!*—I don't, I'm sorry—some writers are that way, whether they express themselves in prose or poetry. In Italy, Pascoli, Gadda, and Landolfi are *writers of meanings*. For them, the word serves to indicate a precise meaning, and is indeed the meaning itself, which by itself is indescribable, undefinable. If you seek to define it you end up destroying it, as Shelley said about the rose, which, 'if blighted, denies the fruit and the seed.' *Writers of words* are of a different breed: they think in *sentences*. The meaning stems from the sum of the words, the relations that words establish with each other: taken individually they say very little, because they need the others to signify. For other writers—Woolf, Stendhal, T.E. Lawrence—the meaning emerges from the chain of relations between words, from the discourse, and these writers, unlike the others, require a listener. They require answers. For the first type, the meanings themselves are answers! Every word, for writers of words, has meaning because it is connected to another word—and not to just any word. Every word has a predisposition to sympathize with one word rather than another. Every word has its own destiny, which is fulfilled in the sentence. And a word doesn't function only in the construct of the sentence. It also functions in relationship to certain hidden words that are not written down, invisible words like ghosts, impalpable but as present as shadows: words that have already been written by someone else and now are evoked by the words that we put down on paper. There are sentences, chains of words that ripple beneath the surface of the page and descend into remote depths where our conscience is unable to plunge, even in moments of great acuity. The *writers of words* are actually readers. The writers of meanings are more similar to scientists, anatomists, or botanists. They catalog. The others collect and forget to classify their findings, because they prefer to scatter around the house whatever they come up with, even at the risk of losing something—what an enviable freedom! *If only I . . .*"

After a long pause, she related that when she was young, when she lived in India, she had compiled a dictionary of the English language. She revealed this to me almost accidentally, without dramatizing this extraordinary confession, as if it had escaped her. I begged her to tell me more.

"The children of the village needed a study aid ..." she started to explain, shrugging her shoulders, "as well as a few *ideas* ..." When she uttered the word "ideas," she suddenly came alive. "Writing a dictionary even for the ordinary purposes I had assigned myself was an immense enterprise!" she said, jumping to her feet. "A most wonderful enterprise! You have the eyes of the past and the future upon you ... I was obviously not the first person to try my hand at one: over the centuries other individuals—not that many, in the end—tried to gather all the words in a book, with only the help of a copyist ..." She approached the tall walnut bookshelf and started to flip randomly through her *Webster*'s. "And, let us not forget, I was a woman, making my enterprise all the more exceptional. A woman who collects and defines words! Unprecedented! Yet a legend tells us that it was a woman who invented the Latin alphabet: Carmenta, the mother of Turnus, Aeneas' enemy ... Sometimes I think the Trojans are like the Jews and the Romans are like the Arabs ... The Egyptian god of writing was also a woman. You can't imagine the kind of people who occupy themselves with gathering the lexical heritage of a nation! You find the strangest characters. Can you believe that one of the most prolific contributors to the *Oxford English Dictionary*, that monument to British lexicography, the dictionary of all dictionaries, was criminally insane, literally—and what's more, an American! I won't tell you his fate ... The same fate as Attis, from the poem by Catullus! He was eventually deported to America, where I visited his grave."

She sat back down and spoke to me about Doctor Johnson, about the hoary-haired James Murray, about a word that was not included in the first edition of the *Oxford English Dictionary* because a slip of paper—on which the entry had been written—fell behind a pile of books ... She told me that she wanted to imitate the style of Doctor Johnson, although her own goals were quite different. In fact, the perpetuation of the English language and its phonetic and semantic stabilization mattered little to her. What mattered to her was the circulation of a few essential *ideas*, and she knew that once these *ideas* began to spread, they would make her dictionary perfectly useless, in the same way that a magic formula becomes useless once it has performed the intended transformation.

"And where is it?" I asked her.

"What? My dictionary? ... I have no clue ... Lost somewhere, I suppose."

I told her we had read some articles from the "Corriere della sera" at school. Signorina Salma believed that newspapers were even more important than books, because they tell you how life really is.

"Nonsense!" the Maestra thundered. "Journalism is the death of thinking and language, Luca. What do journalists do? They create opinions. *Doxa*, as the ancient Greeks called it. We shouldn't listen to them. We don't need opinions! *We need ideas!* ... We need *para*-doxa, the opposite of opinions! Are you following me?" Here she paused for an instant, then, smiling, she resumed her explanation as if a revelation was at hand. "I stopped reading newspapers at an early age and, following in the footsteps of my friend Herodotus, I went out into the world to see how it turns and what *ideas* move it ... And I saw what no newspaper could ever report ... We need dictionaries, not newspapers ..."

She was deep in thought. A shadow passed over her face.

"Dictionaries are everything, Luca," she resumed, solemnly. "Everything! I'm not exaggerating ... What is history if not a collection of words? The words we have been repeating for centuries, or perhaps for only a few years. The important thing is to realize that words do not belong to one person in particular, they belong to everyone. Only the poets, the great writers, have the power to restore the quality of something exclusive to the work—a personal asset. '*Sempre caro mi fu quest'ermo colle*'—So dear to me was this lonely hill. Everyone knows Leopardi's *L'infinito* by heart, or at least they should. Let's take 'ermo'—was there ever a word that was more typical of him? But Leopardi knew that words weren't private property. We all borrow them. Even Leopardi. Even Shakespeare, who invented so many of them. *Comunque*, he took many of his words from the language of the people. The fact that they make their first appearance in the English language in his works does not make them his exclusive property. For example, the word 'accommodation' appears for the first time in *Othello*, but it was already being spoken." After a short pause, she added, her eyes growing moist, "Dictionaries teach us democracy. They've taught you what democracy is at school, haven't they?"

"Yes ..." I answered.

"And what have they taught you? ... No one can understand the deeper meaning of the word 'democracy' if they don't love their language. The meaning of democracy grows out of the love of the languages we speak and the languages we learn ... 'To be one of the many' ... I wouldn't know how else to define it ... This is what democracy is ... Do you understand?"

"Yes ..."

"So it means 'also being one of the others'—'being another.' It's difficult but not impossible. I've spent my whole life trying to think of myself as different from what I am, trying to *become what I am*. Do you understand?"

"Yes ..."

I continued to answer yes, although I understood less and less. I mouthed her words to myself, more enthralled by her passion than what she was trying to explain.

"Let me go over this more carefully, I would hate for you to misunderstand. Democracy is the condition that enables us to be ourselves, to experience—without hurting others—all the instincts that are inside us. Men are evil, Luca, this much is certain—may Machiavelli be forever glorified for establishing this truth once and for all—but people can live together in peace, and even pass themselves off as good, if they find that special condition that transforms their instincts into positive energy. Flaubert wrote a beautiful book about the risks of desiring to be someone else, of reshaping yourself according to impossible images of happiness." She got up to take a volume from the bookshelf. "Madame Bovary would have been a perfect fascist: she wants to be someone else, but not just one of the others. She wants to become someone different from everyone else, different from what she might have become if she had followed her own nature rather that her absurd image of society. Am I making any sense?"

I said yes again, but I could barely find my way through the many contradictory definitions of a single word. Not to mention that I had never read *Madame Bovary*.

"Let me give you an example." The Maestra tried to explain. "One day, when I was a little girl, my grandfather took me to visit a wonderful garden in Cornwall. We found an immense aviary for owls. There were owls of every size and color. Although they were in the bright sunlight they didn't seem to mind: they kept their big yellow or orange eyes wide open, with an air of enigmatic, slightly annoyed wakefulness. Some of them were nesting amid the branches in the far corners of the cage, and you could hardly make them out, those emblems of Olympic indifference. Or wisdom. And—horror of horrors—on the floor of the cage was their meal: piles of dead chicks. But the owls didn't touch them—they wouldn't even look at them. They were waiting for the night, I suppose. But the flies were already feasting. And there, standing in front of those poor slaughtered chicks, tossed together in a macabre heap that erased the physical individuality of each one, I tried to picture the scene of the massacre. How did the aviary keepers kill them? With poison? There weren't any signs of blood or violence. The chicks were simply lifeless, dangling, deflated—hundreds, thousands of chicks if you counted all the cages. I thought: what pleasure can owls get out of gorging on such a mess of carcasses? I imagined legions of soft chirping innocent little chicks scattering to every corner of the cage, running from one part to the other, in search of a non-existent shelter, while the owls swooped down on them. Yes, that's how I would've fed the owls. It's nature's way. The owl is a predator: you have to let it live its life. First, don't lock it in a cage. It's not right for us to appropriate its place and functions. But man never misses an opportunity to usurp the place of someone, even a neighbor. People have forgotten that everyone has his own life, his own being! Sometimes *we ourselves* are the first to renounce this and let others speak or decide for us, including our friends. What are friends if not vampires—enemies on a par with parents, husbands, children? *Friendly advice!*" she snickered. "When I think back to the time in my life when I was drowning in it! And how much it pained me when advice took the form of criticism! But advice is criticism, Luca! No one wants you to be *you*, Luca. They all expect you to be different. And so we grow up with the idea that the way we're living is wrong: we don't even like our own bodies, and yet we come to expect something different from our neighbors—different behaviors, different manners, different words … And maybe it's right, because in the end we know—yes, however vaguely and uncertainly we soooooooo deeply know—there is no one, no one at all in the world who is completely what he or she is supposed to be … *Che tragedia!*… But I digress. I only meant to say that we are like owls in a cage, Luca, digestive machines whose nutritional instincts have been removed, and I don't mean the mere act of feeding ourselves. After that visit I reduced the amount of food I consumed to the bare minimum. That same evening I skipped dinner and the next morning I skipped breakfast. I would have stopped eating entirely if it weren't for the fact that it would lead to my death. But I wanted to live! *Vita*: what a wonderful word! So I started to eat the least amount necessary to avoid dying. And that is how I have lived, day after day, one step away from death, seeing it waiting for me on the opposite shore, separated from me by a glass of water, a slender rivulet. I could even give up the tiny amount that I do ingest, why not? All I can say for myself is that I have not lived by virtue of my daily bread ... I am a cactus, Luca. A desert plant. Do you know what's inside a dead cactus?"

She suddenly turned pale. She realized she had said too much.

She opened the book, in which she had kept her finger the whole time, read a few lines in silence, and out of her mouth came the words: "*Ridicula sum.*"

The last envelopes came in, along with a few more Christmas cakes. The package from the landlord, Signor Spinelli, arrived right on time, and true to a long tradition, it contained a bottle of Prosecco, a pandoro, and a card that read, "Merry Christmas and a Happy New Year to you and your family."

While my mother counted her haul, my father and I started decorating the Christmas tree in the lobby. Until last year trimming the tree had been one of my favorite things, but now it had lost its appeal and actually irritated me. In a single move I managed to shatter three ornaments. My father yelled at me to go away—I was only making a mess. Mother, too busy with her calculations to reprimand me, said to look through the top drawer and replace the three ornaments I had broken with some old woolen pom-poms. As the finishing touch, we hung two strings of flickering Christmas lights over the doorframe and around the window.

At two o'clock sharp we closed up.

My father went out for a walk. My mother started to make the pasta, folding the eggs into flour.

"When I was a little girl, Christmas was a real holiday!" she started reminiscing. "A holiday for the stomach! All we ever got every other day was a boring meal—a plate of spaghetti or vegetables—that was supposed to keep us going until we went to bed at night. But on Christmas we would stuff ourselves. On Christmas Eve we would eat zeppoles, eel, and roasted cod with cooked greens. On Christmas Day we would have tagliolini or raviolini in brodo, and lamb or pork roast. We never touched cow—like Indians—cows were needed for milk. There was a mountain of sweets: torrone, dried figs, chocolate cookies, almond cookies, chickpea cookies ... For a few days our misery would vanish. Never again have I seen such abundance, not even in Milan, when I started working for the Oreficis. The only thing those cheapskates fed me was bread and water! When I think about it ... Well, Chino, your mother was always unlucky. As a child and a teenager I was stuck with my father, that old drunk, and in Milan I learned how mean the rich can be. At least my father was illiterate, poor devil. But the Oreficis? Did I ever tell you about the time ..."

Of course she had, not once but three, four, ten times, and not just on Christmas.

Encouraged by my silence, she started. "He was a doctor and she was a teacher. At least they taught me how to speak properly ..." (in the meantime she kept feeding the dough into the pasta machine). "The lady of the house had decided that she wanted her husband to go to bed with me ... they wanted a child, but she was well along in her years. Every night he tried to get into my room, but I locked the door. At one point I saw the door handle rotating downward. And then he would call out to me, pleading. It was awful. He would go on for half an hour—as if I was the master and he was the servant! But I never gave in. The next day he would act as if nothing had happened and ignore me completely ... Can you believe it? He destroyed me with indifference, while she treated me like a slave, constantly humiliating me ... and she gave me nothing to eat."

She took the pastry wheel and started to cut the ribbons of pasta dough into squares.

"Did you hear that!"

Suddenly we could hear a loud rumbling of voices.

We went up to the second floor. A cluster of people were gathered in front of the Malfitanos' door.

"What happened?" my mother asked.

"Signora Malfitano was attacked by the parrot and is fighting with her husband," Signorina Terzoli reported.

The parrot wouldn't stop screeching, "You were asking for it! You were asking for it!"

"On Christmas Eve of all days!" exclaimed Signora Rovigo. "They don't even have respect for the holidays!"

Vezzali took Malfitano's defense. Ever since that damn bird arrived, the poor woman hasn't had a moment's peace—it was hardly the first time she'd been attacked by the parrot.

My mother was worried about the marble floors. All of those people were destroying her hard work. "Wouldn't you know it, I'll have to go over the whole thing again with the buffer—on Christmas Eve of all days!"

I looked up but she wasn't there. Not even all this screeching had induced her to come out. No, the Maestra remained in her retreat, alone in her apartment, high above, sovereign. As Olympian as the owls in her story.

The snow had already blanketed the stairs and the pine grove. It fell at a regular pace, thick and dry.

My father had on a blazer and tie, my mother a dark dress that Signora Dell'Uomo had given her a few years ago, with a smattering of sequins around the hem and the neckline. "How does it look on me?" she asked. It was the first time she was wearing it.

"You look like a real signora," my father teased her.

We picked up the baking dishes full of food and headed to the building next door. My mother struggled to walk in the snow. She held onto me, afraid she might fall, and shivered from the cold because her dress was too light and her overcoat wasn't long enough. "What the hell is going on back there?" my father exclaimed while we were going through the gate.

"I'll wait for you at Gemma's," she said, without turning around.

At the other side of the garden, some of the tenants had assembled around the fountain to pray. Each of them held a lit candle in their left hand, while their right was cupped around the flame to keep it from being snuffed out by the snowflakes. Pale, motionless, with their faces illuminated from below, they looked like a gathering of the dead. The seamstress was there, too. Signora Dell'Uomo's husband officiated. On behalf of the whole apartment complex he invoked the name of Christ the Savior, beseeching him to protect those present and their loved ones, granting health and prosperity to everyone, and easing the difficult road that lay ahead. "Blessed be the day that Christ the Savior was born!" he intoned. And the others behind him repeated, "Blessed be the day that Christ the Savior was born!"

"Clowns!" my father jeered. "I've got a better idea, Chino, let's go eat."

In addition to us, Gemma had also invited Carmen and her husband. Her boss had granted her the use of the conference room on the ground floor for this special occasion. We occupied only one end of the long table, which was barely covered by the tablecloth.

I wasn't hungry. Instead of eating, I looked through the big picture windows at the falling snow and thought about the Maestra. How much more I wanted to be with her! Although I tried hard not to cry, my cheeks were moist with tears. Luckily no one noticed. My parents and their friends were only paying attention to the food and the conversation. The women complimented each other's recipes and gossiped about the other people in the buildings. The men told dirty jokes freely, as if I couldn't understand.

Once the first course was over, I stood up with the excuse that I had to go to the bathroom. I went to the end of the hall and snuck down the cellar staircase. The lights were off, but from outside, the reflection of the streetlights shone through the high grating. I was terrified, but I had no intention of returning, of sitting back down, of pretending to be cheerful. I curled up between two piles of boxes and, after having a good cry, fell asleep.

I was awoken by music. I didn't know how much time had passed. Maybe an hour. I went back upstairs and into the conference room. The table had been pushed against the wall and the men were in the middle of the room, dressed up like women and dancing. Leaning against the opposite wall, the women were clapping their hands. My father seemed to be enjoying himself the most. He wiggled his ass and the fake breasts, twirling around and around. The other two men aped his movements. What embarrassed me the most, even more than my father's dancing, was my mother's enthusiasm. She pointed at his naked thighs and laughed so hard she had to hold her sides. Gemma and Carmen were also gesturing toward their husbands' hairy legs and almost competing, breathlessly, to see who could laugh the loudest. Roaring with laughter, they threw orange peels and twisted napkins at their husbands' crotches. I thought to myself, "If the Maestra could see us now …"

Before midnight we collected our baking dishes because my mother wanted to go to mass. My father protested that he was tired, but eventually he gave in.

In church we had to find room in the back, in the last available spots. After we were seated, we realized that the pew in front of us was occupied by the Rovigos and the Paolinis, and we hadn't spoken to them since the day that Rita had fallen in the fountain. My father was so tense he couldn't listen to a word of the sermon. A second before the Sign of Peace he tried to escape, but my mother held him back by his coattails. "Stay where you are," she whispered into his ear, "the last thing we need is to feel like we're not even free in the house of the Lord!"

Padre Aldo commanded, "The time has come to exchange a sign of peace," and the Rovigos and Paolinis shook each others' hands. When they turned around to shake the hand of the persons behind them, they were startled to find themselves facing the doorwoman's family. For a second I thought they would turn back around, but they didn't. Once they got over their surprise, they extended their hands to us. But they did not look us in the face. Nor did they say, "Peace be with you."

"This year you have to come with me," my father insisted. My mother didn't want to hear about it. What was wrong with him? He'd always gone by himself. She didn't care for the movies. To spend all that time in the dark, surrounded by strangers ... she wouldn't dream of it! She would rather stay home, safe and sound, watching television. Why throw money away on the movies?

"I'll take you to see a nice film, *The Scientific Cardplayer*, with Bette Davis and Alberto Sordi. You'll like it, you'll see," he promised. "Can't I ask you this one small favor? Or is 'no' the only word in your vocabulary?"

For the first time ever, on December 25, 1972, I saw my parents go out together like a normal couple.

I went upstairs to the fifth floor. Finally I could see the Maestra again. I rapped my knuckles on the door three times. No answer.

I went back home and poured myself a shot of grappa. I took one sip and spat it out. After wetting my lips two or three times, I poured the rest down the sink. I filled our little bathtub to the top with hot water and lowered myself in, hugging my knees and leaning my lower back against the bottom. I felt the hot water grazing my nostrils and I reminisced about the Maestra's lessons. I imagined English words being written in white light on the screen of my lowered eyelids and bleeding out into my memories and thoughts ... The glass door started to shake.

"Who is it?" I cried out, startled.

A hoarse voice asked for my mother.

"She's not in," I replied. "She went to the movies with my father ..." I emphasized the word 'movies' out of spite. A few seconds of

silence followed. I got out of the tub and approached the door, dripping wet. Mantegazza was standing there waiting for me to open, but
I didn't move or say a word. "Tell your mother that last night Signora
Armanda departed," she said. I thought to myself, "So what? Who
cares? She can go wherever she wants . . ." She realized that I hadn't
understood.

"Signora Armanda died last night."

This was followed by the click of the main door. From the window, through an opening in the curtain, I saw Mantegazza weighted
down with trash bags, waddling in her yellow fur coat toward the
dumpster. I suddenly felt a desperate longing for the Maestra. For the
first time I thought that she, too, might die and abandon me forever.
I turned the intercom back on and called her. Still no answer.

When they got home my parents were arguing. "You women are all
alike!" my father shouted. "Nothing is ever good enough for you.
And whose fault is it? The husband's, of course, who else?"

"Of course," my mother protested. "Don't tell me you thought
that idiot Sordi was right! He was the ruin of that poor woman."

"Look, if they lost everything, it's because Mangano decided to
keep on playing. She still wasn't satisfied after cheating the old lady
out of all that money!"

My mother shrugged her shoulders. "Whatever you say. In her
place I would have left immediately! She was right to ask for help from
Modugno, who is a much better man—one hundred percent better!"

"Modugno lost just as much at cards as Sordi, if not more. You
didn't get the meaning of the film. The old lady represents the bosses.
You can never beat the bosses. You can never put them in their place.
Otherwise you turn into a boss yourself, just like them, and the injustice remains. And you've become the oppressor!"

"Better an oppressor than a beggar! . . . And I'd make a better boss than the old lady. Sometimes I wonder how much of a communist you are. As far as you're concerned, things should never change."

When I heard them mention the old lady in the film, I remembered the news Mantegazza gave me. "The old lady died!" I hollered. My father turned two questioning eyes on me. "Our old lady!" I clarified. "Signora Armanda! She's dead!"

My mother turned pale. "The old lady died?"

My father burst into laughter, having grasped the misunderstanding. "So, the old lady died," he repeated to himself. "That old fascist is dead."

My mother expected us to go upstairs with her. In the event of a tenant's death, she claimed, her professional duties required that we, too, the family of the custodian, had to participate in the expression of condolences.

My father muttered the word "condolences" between gritted teeth, and went straight back home. I stayed behind with my mother. There was no one in the apartment except for the younger Mantegazza, their dog Bella, and the deceased, who had been laid out on the large double bed. Not even death had managed to tame the shrewish expression furrowing the skin between her almost invisible eyebrows. The dog howled from its prone position on the sheepskin rug near the bed.

"Poor Signora Armanda! Did she suffer?" my mother asked.

"Hardly!" said Mantegazza—perfectly coifed and made up—without the least emotion, as if she were reporting a news story she'd heard on TV. "This morning I got up, prepared breakfast, and called out to her. I went in the bedroom to see because she didn't answer. She was already cold. The doctor thinks she died last night, after going to bed. At one point, I heard her gasp for air. That's when she must have died. In my opinion, it was indigestion from the Christmas cake. It's really awful, the panettone they make nowadays ... when I was a little girl, it had a completely different taste ..."

"You're right," my mother agreed, although she had never laid eyes on panettone when she was growing up.

Mantegazza asked her to prepare the body for the priest's visit and started to hand her a ten-thousand-lira bill. "I wouldn't think of it," my mother protested, taking a step back. "I was really fond of Signora Armanda!"

Mantegazza waved her hands impatiently, in her theatrical manner, as if she was drying the money in the air. "Come on—take the money! I don't want to argue."

Without wasting a moment, my mother undressed the body and gave it a sponge bath. She noticed there was no hair between the dead woman's legs. Amused, she said that Miss Armanda had reverted to being a little girl. The corpse didn't bother her in the least. She dressed it in nice clothes and painted its sunken cheeks and lips with a little rouge. "We really are nothing but dust," she commented while arranging the curls over the corpse's gray forehead.

Padre Aldo arrived close to suppertime. He lit a candle, said a prayer, and blessed the remains. He didn't linger because he was expected back at six o'clock for the Christmas greetings. Mantegazza extended a banknote that quickly disappeared into his outstretched hand. "This is the first time I've blessed a deceased person on Christmas Day," he observed. And at the door, he asked me, "Why have you stopped going to Mass?"

At Mantegazza's request, my mother also handled the funeral arrangements. She took care of every detail, from the floral wreaths to the vestments to the transportation. Meanwhile the dog sniffed at her feet and, growling, bared its few remaining teeth.

The body remained in the house for almost a week, laid out on the bed just as my mother had arranged it. To get rid of the smell, Mantegazza smoked like a chimney. At night she slept on a sofa in the living room, although she deeply regretted—so she said—leaving her poor mother all alone in that big bed.

Early in the afternoon of the 31st, the coffin was closed and loaded into the hearse. The undertakers had wanted to lay the coffin out on a bier in the lobby, but my mother said absolutely not. The signore would've taken it as a bad omen—on the last day of the year, no less!

Besides the seamstress and her daughter Rosi, only my mother and I went to the church. No one else from the apartment complex came. The minibus that Signora Mantegazza had rented for the tenants was sent back to the garage, unused. Not even her relatives were there, unless you considered the dog a relative. It took up a post right below the head of the coffin, and was a little more vigilant than usual. Next to the coffin were wreaths from the other tenants, from Mantegazza herself, and from the director of the swimming pool where she worked.

The seamstress wore a mangy raccoon coat that we had seen, years earlier, on the old woman. Her gestures and expressions reeked of servility: she was clearly counting on getting a share of the deceased's estate. And while enticing the old lady with cups of coffee, she must have discovered that the coat hadn't been left to us.

During the religious service, Rosi couldn't sit still for a minute. She kept running from one end of the church to the next, throwing the pews into disarray, and snuffing out the candles. My mother watched her, stifling her laughter. Mantegazza, despite her annoyance, tried to pay attention to the words of Padre Aldo, who had the good sense to keep the service down to the essentials. At the moment of benediction, the seamstress faked a sob. Mantegazza did not even deign to look at her. My mother was seized by an uncontrollable euphoria. To avoid bursting into laughter, she had to bend herself in two and groan. Not to be outdone, the seamstress unleashed another torrent of tears. Mantegazza continued to ignore her, while my mother seemed to be overwhelmed with grief.

Outside the church, Mantegazza asked if we wouldn't mind following her to the cemetery. The question, which sounded more like a command, caught both my mother and the seamstress off-guard. For the first time they looked each other in the eye, as if they were both wondering how they could escape this unexpected burden and, calling a momentary truce, came to a mutually beneficial agreement: in the end, without a sound, they both got into the big black Mercedes.

We rode through streets I had never seen, sad and gloomy, impervious to the Christmas lights. Until then I had imagined the city was more beautiful beyond the fields surrounding Via Icaro, beyond the gates enshrouded in fog. I was wrong.

Because of the cold, the priest at the cemetery also limited himself to the essentials. A moment before the gravediggers started to cover the grave, the seamstress told her daughter, "Rosi, take a clump of dirt and throw it on *nonna*." The little girl, figuring *nonna* was the older woman standing in front of her rather than the one lying in the grave, grabbed a handful of soil and threw it at Mantegazza. "Good God!" the woman shouted, jumping to one side. "Signora Bortolon, a little respect! Don't you realize I'm burying my mother?"

My mother giggled, and I giggled with her. The seamstress gave Rosi a slap across the face. "Apologize to Signorina Mantegazza!" she hollered. The only thing you could hear in the cemetery was her strident voice. The little girl fled through the deserted grave-stones, which were dappled with the remaining snow. Handfuls of dirt were scattered onto the casket. Without thinking, Mantegazza, after a long final drag, tossed her cigarette butt into the pit.

"How old was Signora Armanda?" asked the seamstress, unremitting in her gall. Mantegazza blew smoke through her nostrils and chewed on her lower lip with an absent look while the gravediggers finished their work. I thought she hadn't heard the question. "It was a secret," she said after a long pause, staring into space. "Momma was against anyone knowing—but what's the sense of secrets anymore? She was ninety."

"What a woman!" crowed the seamstress, "to make it all the way to ninety. That I should be so lucky!"

"She was here not even ten minutes ago," my father remarked, "the Maestra—and what a character! She can't weigh more than eighty pounds."

The gift-wrapped packages were placed on top of the television set. From their shape you could tell they were books. I could imagine which ones. The biggest package was her *Webster's*. The second was her copy of *Madame Bovary*, in French. On the title page she had written, "For Luca, Happy New Year!" Her holiday wish for me was a warning, not to lose my bearings amid the myriad false idols I would encounter.

"Can I go upstairs to thank her?" I asked my mother.

"You'll thank her later, she knows you're spending the holidays with your parents . . ."

We had nothing planned for the evening. Gemma and Carmen were going to a pizzeria with their husbands. My mother didn't have the least intention of wasting her money, especially since her own pizza was so good. Nor, for that matter, did she feel like leaving the building unguarded on the last night of the year, with fireworks going off everywhere and a bunch of drunk men on the prowl. "If anything happens, you know who they're going to blame."

We turned on the television and sat down to eat. The front door kept slamming as people came and went as if it were a regular work day—a constant reminder that everyone was out merrymaking except us. Even the Vignolas were having fun.

We made the dinner last for as long as possible so it would look as if we, too, were celebrating New Year's. The menu was elaborate.

My father had requested chicken soup, pig's feet and lentils, an assortment of side-dishes, and gorgonzola with walnuts, one of his favorites. My mother let a few minutes go by between one course and the next, and she asked us to eat slowly. How would we make it to midnight, otherwise?

By ten o'clock, my father was so tired he could barely keep his eyes open. My mother was sleepy, too, but she forced herself to stay awake. There was still the dried fruit and the canned peaches. And the coffee ... to be capped off by a toast, with the bottle of Prosecco the landlord had sent, and the panettone. But my father wanted to eat the panettone right away, and then have a cup of coffee. My mother, following the order she'd established, opened the can of peaches and served them to him. He still wanted panettone, so she dropped a rough wedge onto his plate. She and I would have our servings later.

The feast was over.

My father disappeared into the bedroom. After washing the dishes and helping me to open up the bed, my mother joined him. She set the alarm clock for eleven fifty-five so we could all get up to toast the New Year together. Otherwise our wishes wouldn't come true.

I closed my eyes and pressed Flaubert's novel to my chest. In that position, with a book I still couldn't read, I was finally able to survey the room more serenely: the gas meter, the window, the sliding bolt lock, the key drawer, the intercom, all the knickknacks you wouldn't find in a normal home, and all the protrusions that hindered our movements and freedom. Suddenly they no longer felt oppressive, wrong, and unsightly, but rather provisional, as provisional as the people carousing upstairs and the fireworks going off in the fields.

At midnight we opened the bottle from the landlord and drank a toast to the New Year. My father gave me a kiss on the cheek and drew my mother toward him. She broke away from his embrace impatiently, raising the glass to an audience that only she could see.

"Happy New Year! *Auguri!* Happy 1973! The time has finally come for us to buy a house, too! Happy New Year! Viva the new house! Viva 1973!"

My father didn't have the courage to contradict her, so he stroked her hair tenderly. And she continued, rebelliously, "Happy New Year! Viva 1973! Viva the new house!"

After the holidays Miss Lynd also gave us an envelope. We really weren't expecting it, and inside was a ten-thousand-lira note, compensation for all the help my mother had given her. At the sight of the money, my mother was puzzled. The gift cheered her up—it was cash, after all—but she was also a little offended. She would have preferred to keep the Maestra in her debt. "No one's going to buy me," she said.

She had become jealous. She realized that the Maestra was transforming me. I had stopped watching television and my nose was always in a book. I spoke in a strange way and often used words that to her were unknown, incomprehensible, even foreign . . . She appreciated the change in me, since it came from the time I was spending with an exceptional person, but she also disapproved, since it had made us grow apart. Her problems and dreams no longer interested me. I had stopped participating in her long vigil for the sale of the building, and, sharing her hopes that we would soon be taking over the Vignolas' one-bedroom apartment. I had already found a new home. It was on the fifth floor of the building, not the first. And it was filled with books. And English was the language spoken there.

The money had to be returned. But thinking long and hard about the matter, she decided to keep it, since the purchase of a home remained an absolute priority. On the intercom she thanked the Maestra and said that, to reciprocate, besides the usual weekly cleaning, she would start ironing her linens. The Maestra told her there was no need. She didn't iron anything, much less the linens. Ironing was a waste of time. All one had to do was hang them out properly while they were still wet.

"Thank goodness not everyone thinks like your Maestra," my mother said, "how in the world would I make a living otherwise!"

The following Sunday, when she went upstairs to clean, the Maestra sent her away. Thank you, she said, but she would no longer be requiring her services.

Once school started, my English lessons would also resume. My mother could no longer use the holidays as an excuse to keep me from going upstairs. I returned to the fifth floor with renewed enthusiasm. Every day I collected dozens of unknown words and definitions, copying them into my notebook, which slowly filled up with my handwriting. At night, before turning out the light, I would reread the words to memorize them, but also in an effort to go beyond the threshold of sleep and beyond the pleasure I had felt in the afternoon.

In a passage from my textbook we came across the word *God*. Having ascertained that I knew the meaning, the Maestra asked me to define it. It was customary for me to give her either a description or a synonym (although, according to the Maestra, there were no true synonyms—were there perfect equivalents for *life, time, air, flower* ... ?). An example would be even better. But never, ever, should I provide a translation. Dumbfounded, I sat there in silence. Happier than if I'd given her an answer, she took my silence for the indisputable proof that God did not exist.

"*Very good!* One can hardly expect to define such a ridiculous term. Every language has a certain number of such words: meaningless words that belong to the realm of religion. Of course, if you look it up in a bilingual dictionary, you find *Dio*. So what? There are languages in which the concept of divinity is completely absent. In Hebrew—the language of the people of God!—the word exists, but you're not supposed to utter it ... An old friend of mine considered *God* to be 'the shortest and ugliest of our mono-syllables.' For me it means something only if you read it backward ..."

I knew the Maestra was critical of priests, but I overlooked the possibility that she might actually be an atheist. I was used to my mother's form of religion, the religion of women who speak to God with the same candor they use to haggle over the price of vegetables at the market. I was convinced that all the mothers of the world—because, in the end, Miss Lynd was a mother, too—shared the same God, an invisible being, creator of heaven and earth, to whom they turned to pray for help. He was also my God. Every night, since childhood, I would say my prayers to him before falling asleep. For years and years I had asked him to give my mother enough money to buy the Vignolas' apartment, and lately I also thanked him in my prayers for bringing the Maestra into my life.

"*Poor Luca*, you obviously believe in God, right?" she surmised, "and in the poor Blessed Mother . . . the Immaculate Conception . . . the Resurrection of the Son . . ." She shook her head, disconsolate. I didn't know what to say. I knew my mother would be very unhappy if she could see me so unprepared to defend the faith. "It's not your fault, *caro Luca*," she persisted. "At school they don't teach you to read the dictionary, but they do teach you that God, with a capital G, is great and good and merciful, that things happen because it is the will of God . . . Your son gets sick and dies, but it is all part of His divine plan. Populations are slaughtered by the millions, yet even this is part of His divine plan. It's so complex! Such PERFECTION! Everything fits into His divine plan: wars, fascism, concentration camps, famine, disease, social injustice, unemployment, fratricide, the exploitation of children! Yesterday I went to the young people at the Home for the Disabled to wish them a Happy New Year. Have you ever been there? . . . You should go! It would force you to realize the unimaginable sophistication of the divine plan: bodies without arms, heads with one eye, tongues that are ten inches long, giant skulls, no ears, no legs, no torso! One patient is dragging himself around, another is slithering, and yet another is jumping like a grasshopper. Many of them don't move at all, and only scrunch up their faces. As for words, no one knows how to speak. They make sounds, yes, and they're very good at it! Shrieks, moans, gasps, gurgling, whinnying, hiccupping. What a concert! What a show! The joyous beauty of the *divine plan*! Why not? Let us give thanks to God for all this! Whom else—seeing that there's no one to thank? ... God is *no one*! When will people wake up and realize this?" Her indignation propelled her from her armchair, back and forth across the small room, which swelled with her spirit, expanded into a cosmic stage. "God is a beautiful fairy tale. God can do everything. For children he's a kind of wizard, a witch doctor! He moves mountains, resuscitates the dead ... is there anything your God can't do?" She heaved a sigh and her sarcasm gave way to melancholy. "I have never been a believer. I have always been strange, ever since I was little. And unhappy—a very unhappy girl! Was it because I didn't have God in my life? I don't think so. People don't know what to do with someone like me. I've often ended up alone because of my ideas, and I'm not talking about voluntary solitude—that's another matter, which I've allowed to grow inside me like a garden. In Latin there's a good word for it, *secretum*. Did they teach you that in school? ... I'm talking about another kind of solitude, the kind you don't choose, the kind that threatens to turn your garden into a desert. I'm talking about abandonment ... And one day you will abandon me, too—won't you, my sweet Luca? If you abandon me, I'll understand ... I'm crazy!"

The Maestra uttered these last words with a sob and turned her head in the other direction, where there was still a little daylight.

"Luca, I'm sorry! ... I'm crazy! Do you know the first word written in the first English dictionary? You don't? ... *Abandon* ... you will abandon me, Luca. You, too." Then she called herself an idiot, because her tirade had ruined everything. She laughed desperately, and I laughed with her, because I was fond of her and couldn't stand the idea of losing her.

"You are crazy, too," she concluded with a comic grin, wiping away a stubborn tear with the tip of her little finger. "Otherwise you would've already stopped coming here. But instead you come to see me every day. A young boy visiting an old lady ... Unheard of ... only in fairy tales, like God ... I must tell your mother ... Elvira, has Luca seen a doctor? If I were your mother I'd be worried. Why do you come here? You should be running around in the courtyard, playing with children your own age ..."

She brushed aside the voile curtains and cast an almost cruel gaze across the street, where a group of boys was chasing a soccer ball on the muddy ground, illuminated by the Christmas lights.

"Yes, you are crazy, too, Luca. Life is going to be a journey through the ruins for you, too ..."

She'd never worked harder in her life, doing people's ironing, cleaning apartments, knitting wool sweaters and trying to sell them. At night, after my father went to bed, she would work on the multicolored blanket that sat heavily on her lap like a shaggy dog, billowing out in waves onto the floor.

She imagined that Aldrovanti would make the announcement with a very formal telephone call, or maybe in person. The sale of the *establishment*—how she loved saying that word! So much finer than "the building" or "the complex," because it lent the seal of bureaucracy to her fantasies, conveying both security and durability—*stability*, that was the key, while the other words indicated something vague and confused that didn't suit the long-awaited opportunity of a lifetime. It was hardly an everyday occurrence: Aldrovanti might very well want to speak with her one on one. To prepare for the big event she counted, over and over again, the money she'd managed to set aside. Her bed was covered with financial statements, banknotes, and pieces of paper on which additions and multiplications had been scribbled. Even my birthday savings, tucked away in the tin box, were included in the calculation. I saw her moving her lips silently and raising her eyes to the ceiling in search of a solution. My presence got on her nerves. "Go to the front room!" she would shout, "before some Jehovah's Witness sneaks in. Go on! You're only in my way here!" No matter how many times she counted, she was always a million lira short, but she still hoped that the sale would be announced as early as tomorrow. She was convinced that the missing money would appear out of nowhere, all of a sudden, by magic. *It had to appear!* She had eighty percent of the total, and that was already a lot, a whole lot.

From the depths of the armoire she dug out her checkbook and stared at it in disbelief, already savoring the moment when she would tear off the first check to write in the amount of the down payment. The very thought made her dizzy. Would she know how to fill out a check? What if she made a mistake? She'd look like such a fool! Oh, what did it matter. Some saint would rush to her aid. And if she made a mistake writing out the first check, she'd get the second one right . . . she had ten checks total. Plenty to spare!

The first half of January had passed and Aldrovanti still hadn't made the phone call. My mother's nerves were frayed—she prayed to the saints, to God, to the Virgin Mary. Her prayers alternated with curses. She cursed life, the apartment complex, the world . . .

With or without the intercession of some saint, the building manager finally appeared, shortly before the end of the month, accompanied by two consultants. The three of them inspected the building from top to bottom, inside and out. They also went downstairs to the boiler room. Under the stairs Aldrovanti noticed the lair of the gray cat. She wrinkled her nose at the stench of urine and reached back toward the outdoors, as if to grab a last mouthful of breathable air. When she turned around, she knocked over a saucer of leftover milk, brought there by someone or other. All hell broke loose.

She raced up the stairs and started to shout the most offensive words imaginable: saying my mother's neglect had turned the building into a pig pen, that this wasn't a public-housing project, that the landlord would die of a heart attack if he ever laid eyes on such filth! The cat had to go—and immediately! And to think she had told my mother, when she started working there so many years ago, that no cats were allowed in the building! . . . My mother tried in vain to explain that the cat helped keep the mice away, which infiltrated the courtyard from the fields at night. Indeed, one cat was hardly enough . . .

"Oh!" the building manager laughed derisively, lowering her voice but not her contemptuous tone. "So, would you have us turn the building into a kitty mill? Don't talk nonsense, Elvira! We're not in your village anymore. If mice are a problem we call the exterminators! Do you or do you not know your duties? Do I have to write them out for you and tape them to your refrigerator door? And for heaven's sake, get rid of that rag! This is first and foremost the loge, not your kitchen ..."

The consultants determined that the tiles on the rear façade showed signs of deterioration, some had already started to detach from the cement wall, and the possibility could not be excluded that, unless work were done as soon as possible, they might fall. So from then on, no one was to venture into that area.

Aldrovanti's tirade did not keep my mother's spirits depressed for long. What she did mind, however, was that the reason for the visit of this unpleasant, domineering woman wasn't the sale of the building. What if she *was* fooling herself? In fact, if the landlord wanted to sell, why was he so worried about maintenance? That should have been the new owners' problem! ... Or maybe—and here I saw her succumbing to a new illusion—since the landlord, *l'ingegnere*, was a gentleman, a *true* gentleman!—he wanted the building to be in the best possible condition for the sale ... "What more can we do?" she concluded. "Be patient? ... I've been *very* patient, haven't I, sweetheart? Hasn't your mommy been patient? We're almost there ... I can't wait to see the looks on their faces! Their jaws will drop. Ah, yes, my dears. Now I'm an owner, too! Time to go looking for another *doorwoman*! ... And your father had better not try to stop me! If he doesn't back me up on this, I'm going to ask for a divorce. Anyone who thinks that only the rich can afford a divorce has got to be an idiot! I've got money, too—me, a nobody. I don't need anyone! And there's plenty of work to go around! Your father had better watch out! Patience, I just need a little more patience ... Sooner or later the ingegnere is going to sell."

The knitting dropped from her hands. The door would've burst open if it hadn't been held firmly in place by the crossbars.

"Don't move, for the love of God!" she ordered me. Another colossal blow shook the wooden doorframe. The windows of the loge trembled. So did the cups and glasses in the cupboard. The Murano vase skated across the smooth Formica tabletop.

"What the hell is going on?" shouted my father, running out of the bathroom half-naked.

"Quiet!" The pounding stopped.

"It must be some drunk," my mother said, "let's have a look . . ."

"You're not going to open the door, are you?!"

"Let me handle it . . ."

She was already pulling back the bolt. She cautiously opened the door a crack, taking a peek outside, while my father got the longest knife from the table drawer.

"It's Signor Zarchi!"

"Let me see . . ."

My father pushed her to one side and opened the door a little wider. The inarticulate howling continued, getting louder and louder. By now the whole building must've been awake. You couldn't understand a word, only the repetition of a sequence of vowels: "*Ooooia, eee . . .*"

"What the hell is he saying? Is he drunk out of his mind?"

My mother called Signora Zarchi on the intercom.

"Madam, did you hear that noise? Down here, in the lobby, your husband is making a scene. He's drunk as a skunk. Please come get him before something happens," she said, removing the knife from my father's hands and opening the door.

"Hey!" she shouted out, authoritatively, the way you would scold a child.

Startled by that unexpected voice, the enraged hulk of a man quieted down all of a sudden, turned slowly, and made a few shaky steps in my mother's direction. She quickly closed the door and stood looking at him through the window. The poor man started howling again, but he had been placated, at least in part. He could barely stand. His jacket hung down on one side and his shirt was untucked from his dirty wrinkled trousers. He was gasping for air, and in the effort to speak clearly, he twisted his facial features into horrible grimaces, as if he wanted to convey an important message to my mother—and he was making progress, his utterances becoming clearer: the sounds that were indecipherable earlier, the *ooooia*'s and *eeee*'s, started to rearrange themselves gradually into two complete words. *Whoooo, priiiee* . . . The words coming out of his mouth were distorted, but he was clearly saying *Whore* . . . *priest. Whore* . . . *priest. Whore* . . . *priest. Whore* . . . *priest. Whore* . . . *priest. Whore* . . . *priest. Whore* . . . *priest. Whore* . . . *priest.*

"That whore is doing it with the priest!" my father translated, filling in the blanks in the syntax as if he were solving an ancient enigma.

Signora Zarchi arrived in a long pink dressing gown. From the opening of the elevator, she called out timidly to her husband. "Romano . . ."

He turned around and, recognizing her, lost what little reason he seemed to have regained: "WHORE!" is the word that burst out of his heart, through his lips. This time the word echoed loud and clear. Signora Zarchi retreated to the back of the elevator and, before closing the doors—setting aside her normally seraphic air—she begged my mother to have him taken away before he killed her, the animal. The elevator whooshed upstairs. The only thing the jealous husband could do was bang a fist against the frosted glass, through which you could see the rubber pulleys dangling, like a pair of lowered suspenders.

The tenants, who had been leaning over the railings the whole time, started to murmur. Malfitano's parrot suddenly appeared in the stairwell, unleashing ear-splitting shrieks and snatches of prayer, until a call from his mistress brought him back to the second floor. The seamstress, Signora Mellone, and Signora Dell'Uomo collapsed in laughter, partly to ease the tension, partly because they were so amused by the bird's performance. "Just when you thought it couldn't get any worse, out pops the parrot!" Then, perfectly coordinated, Vezzali and Paolini came down the stairs and immobilized Zarchi. He was so debilitated by alcohol and his outburst that even my mother could've tackled him. As soon as the two men took him by the arms, he sagged and ended up on the floor, at the foot of the stairs, as if he had rolled all the way down from the top floor. Signora Mellone suggested they call emergency services. A few minutes later the ambulance arrived. To speed things along, my mother opened the gate, letting the ambulance drive into the courtyard and park by the front stairs. Signora Zarchi came back down, this time with her half-asleep daughter. She had removed her dressing gown and donned a long dark dress. She dispensed her gratitude and apologies to the brood of hens as the emergency workers lifted her husband onto the stretcher. Getting into the ambulance herself, Rita repeated her mother's words, which echoed into the empty night.

By mid-March the stems of the roses were already as tall as me. If you looked carefully, in the midst of the luxuriant foliage you could also find an occasional rosebud. The air was filled with corpuscles, dust, and pollen, clumping together into fuzzy little balls that stuck to the sidewalk. The mud was drying in the fields and the tree branches were growing and adorning themselves with soft bright-green gems and fresh shoots. The hydrangeas were a halo of buds. The gray cat (my mother, ignoring the manager, had thought twice about getting rid of her) sharpened her claws on the bark of trees and wandered through the flower beds on the prowl for birds. At night she howled in heat, with an almost human lament. The children went back outdoors to shriek to their hearts content and the bigger boys played soccer in the field across the street. At night, behind the little hill, now cloaked in a light emerald fuzz, there were more and more cars parked with foggy windows.

My mother was also feeling the warmth of spring: she kept the window open from dawn to dusk, listening to the song of the blackbirds and the whisper of the breeze between the leaves of the sycamore tree. At the enchanting sound—despite the delay in the long-awaited announcement—she would start to daydream: in the new bedroom she would hang curtains like the ones she had seen in the Dell'Uomo apartment, beige with embroidered hems. She would buy any furniture she needed at the factory outlets in Brianza ... There was no need to change the bed and the armoire right away—she could get by with what she had for a little while longer ... But a proper sofa-bed was needed for me, one that could be pulled out with a finger or by simply flicking a switch . . .

Easter Sunday was like summer, and although my father didn't suffer from the heat like my mother, he put on a short-sleeved shirt. The sunlit air billowed in white tufts. "I've never seen a spring like this," my mother exclaimed as we left the church. "Can you smell it? Can you smell the fragrance?" The spring breathed new life into her dreams. The renewal of nature foretold the renewal of her life. Light and joy emanated from her face, as if something amazing had happened to her, as if she had fallen in love . . .

The moment had come for me to choose which high school to attend. The Maestra took it for granted that I would enroll at the Classical Lyceum. But my parents felt a technical school that taught bookkeeping would be more suitable. To my mother the Lyceum sounded too abstract; to my father it sounded ridiculous. What the hell was the point of studying Latin and Greek, two languages that hadn't been spoken for centuries? There was no point whatsoever. It would be a joke, a waste of time and money . . .

One night, after closing, the Maestra came downstairs to the loge to plead her case for the Classical Lyceum. Bewildered by her unexpected visit, my father was completely disarmed by her arguments. He timidly suggested that we were proletarians who couldn't afford to waste money and time on a useless education. She replied that the word proletarian was as old as the law of the twelve tables, the most ancient Roman legislation, and she launched into a praise of etymology and dead languages that left my parents tongue-tied.

The next day she helped me fill out the preregistration form.

"Very good, Luca," she said approvingly, after a final look at the completed application. "Let me be clear about one thing: no school really does its job . . . School is a factory of lies. But a classical education is better than the others. At least you'll learn a few words of ancient Greek. You'll read Thucydides in his own language! Did I ever tell you about the opening of the *Peloponnesian War*? Wait ... now where did I put it?"

She browsed through the volumes on the top shelf and found what she was looking for. She read quietly, to herself, the opening lines of the work in the original, and then she translated it for me, along with other passages from the introduction.

"Beautiful," I said, to gratify her.

She admitted that Thucydides was a very difficult author, and that she wasn't sure if she had understood him herself, even after many re-readings. "A possession for all time ..." she ruminated. And addressing me again: "I wonder whether it is right to expect things to last forever ... Certainly, for love of the truth ... Let me give you an example. In Moscow, in Red Square, the embalmed body of Lenin is on display. You know who he is, don't you? ... I was only able to observe it for a few moments because there was a long line of visitors and the guards refused to allow me enough time for serious contemplation. But those few moments were enough to impress on my memory the unmistakable color of his hair and beard, the yellow pallor of his skin ... At that moment I didn't think about his fame or historic importance—I thought, instead, about the durability of matter, about the physical survival of something that no longer has a direct relationship with the reality around it. Lenin belonged to the past, yet there he was, looking the same as he had when he was alive, as if the dead man before me were not really him but rather everything that had surrounded him when he was still alive. That's what moved me: the solitude of the embalmed body. And what that solitude represented—a self-consciously transient universe that was determined to endure, and had chosen Lenin to represent that era to posterity. Lenin was a remnant, a relic, a trace ... And the others?

Where were his contemporaries? What was the purpose of preserving only one man's body, of spurning the laws of death and becoming not just a contemporary of posterity, but surviving it? ... And what of the mummy of Ramses II, at the Cairo Museum? ... To think that after so many centuries he still bears the face of a despot ... Are you following? ... What is the truth? ... Now it's time for you to go ...”

She was dismissing me earlier than usual. I walked the short distance from the chair to the door, reluctantly picking up my notebooks and the preregistration form. The Maestra held the door handle and added: “Tomorrow there's no need for you to come, Luca. Maybe it would be better if we suspended our afternoon lessons for the time being. It won't hurt you to study by yourself. By now you know what to do. I need my rest. Why the long face? Don't tell me you're offended?” She didn't have a very cheerful expression, either. Speaking to me this way seemed to pain her. “Chin up ... no one has died. Come on! Look at me ...”

My heart stopped. All the bliss of the previous months evaporated in an instant. I cast a final glance around the room where I had spent the happiest hours of my life and then I shuffled outside with the first teardrops welling up in my eyes.

“Luca,” she called to me.

I didn't listen. Why should I? She didn't want me anymore.

Huddled in a corner of the bedroom, I repeated to myself that the Maestra had abandoned me, that she was tired of me ... I had been deceived. The Maestra had played with my feelings—I was just one of her experiments ... The intercom rang. My mother, who was rinsing the vegetables in the sink, shouted at me, "Chino, answer it ... it's the Maestra ... What else does she want? For Pete's sake! You just left three minutes ago!"

She had to take the call herself. "Yes, thank you, Miss Lynd, that'll be fine. Alright. We'll keep your advice in mind."

Hearing my mother enter the room, I stood up and went to the window, turning my back to her. "The Maestra wants us to stop calling you Chino at home. She says that your name is Luca, *'the child of luck'* ... she must be losing her marbles, that one! ..." My mother was shocked. So was I—shocked by the Maestra's determination, until the end, to make sure I became the person I was meant to be. I said nothing. I stared out at the horizon. Any wisp of fog had cleared, and the rows of poplar trees were swaying in the breeze.

During supper I burst into tears.

"Would you mind telling me what's come over you?" my mother asked. "Are you tired? ... The Maestra is putting too much pressure on you! Enough of all that English now! You'll learn it when you're older! Just look what it's doing to you ... Come now, sweetheart, tell me what's wrong? If something's bothering you, you have to tell your mother. Did the Maestra do something to you? ... Did you know," she added, turning to my father, "that she called me on the intercom just to tell me that from now on we should start calling our son Luca instead of Chino? Who does she think she is? First she demands that we send him to the Lyceum. Now she expects us to give him another name ... If she wanted a son so much, why didn't she have one herself?"

"But she's right," my father said, "the boy's name is Luca. Let's try calling him that. Maybe then he'll stop whining like such a sissy ..." He noticed the steak still sitting on my plate, untouched. "Come on, eat!" he ordered me.

"Don't insist!" my mother scolded him. "He'll eat. Don't insist or you'll only make the situation worse." She turned to me: "And you—tomorrow afternoon you stay home. Understood? You're wearing yourself out ... I'm not letting you go up there anymore! And if that woman sticks her nose into things that are none of her business, then I won't send you to the Lyceum, either!"

I got up from the table and said that I was going to walk up and down the stairs to clear my head. I made it up to the fifth floor, counting every step. I headed toward the Maestra's door and started crying again. I could see my reflection in the surface of the polished wood. I hoped the Maestra would hear my sobs, open the door, invite me in and console me, and at one point, yes, I thought I could feel her presence on the other side of the door—a slight sound. She must have noticed something, yes, now she was coming to open up for me ... I was ready to fall to her feet, to beg her to keep me with her forever ... but the door remained closed.

Still in tears, I went down one flight of stairs and looked out from the balcony next to the trash chute. The stench of garbage invaded my nostrils. A white car parked at the foot of the hill and turned its headlights off. In the courtyard the cat was clinging to the sycamore tree, assailed by two claimants. The swallows glided through the sky, catching insects. Paolini and Cavallo had just come through the gate. Riccardo was sitting with his legs crossed on the bench facing the fountain, and next to him was a blonde girl, partly concealed by the wisteria leaves. They were holding each other's hands. I stood there scrutinizing them and, without realizing it, slowly calmed down. The last teardrops dried on my cheeks and turned cold. I was suddenly filled with a kind of serenity, a reassuring melancholy. In my mind's eye I climbed an endless staircase that spiraled up to the stratosphere and I reached the highest floor of the tallest building in the world, like one of those amazing new skyscrapers in New York, the Twin Towers, that I had seen on television recently, and I leapt and let my body float down.

III

The main door slammed with its unmistakable metallic clank. We both looked up, me from my Latin book, she from the pair of overalls she was mending. The moment they appeared behind the door, we knew. Right before standing up my Mom gave me a meaningful glance. The day had arrived. I was reminded of the words in the Gospel: "*Ecce ancilla Domini, fiat mihi secundum verbum tuum*—Behold the handmaid of the Lord, be it done unto me according to thy word." She opened the glass door and greeted them calmly. With an almost imperceptible hand gesture she ordered me to leave.

"Good work, Elvira," came the compliments of the ingegnere, ignoring her hello, "I can see you keep this building so clean you could eat off the floor."

Although she hadn't been forewarned of their visit, the lobby and the loge were sparkling. Finally all her diligence, all that cleaning, was going to pay off. Good work, Elvira. The landlord was there to give her the recognition she was due!

She invited him to have a seat but he preferred to remain standing next to the table. He was very tall with an easy elegance. You could imagine that a trusted servant had prepared him and, after the last stroke of the brush, had approved the image of the master. Even I, through the keyhole, could perceive the sobriety of his posture, which, combined with the undeniable superiority of his rank, lent him a unique appeal.

My mother uttered humbly, "I do my best, Sir."

For fear of looking like an idiot in front of the manager, she displayed the scars on her wrists: "Every day, every morning, even at the cost of my health . . ."

"You don't have an easy job," Ingegner Spinelli acknowledged. "It takes a lot of physical strength. But you're a young and energetic woman, I can see that—strong-willed, resilient, the kind of woman only the South can produce! We're lucky to have you here . . ."

"Elvira is precious," the manager interjected. Next to the tall and debonair landlord, she looked like a midget.

My mother—out of both surprise and a reflexive gratitude— could barely hold back her tears. The ingegnere paid no mind to the doorwoman's show of emotion and without further ado extracted a sheet of paper from his jacket pocket, unfolding it on the table.

"My dear Elvira," he said in a serious tone, signifying the start of a new era. "On this piece of paper you will find, in alphabetical order, the names of the tenants at Via Icaro 15. Can you see? Biondo, Bortolon, Caselli, Cavallo, D'Antonio, Dell'Uomo, Di Lorenzo, Lojacano, Lynd . . . Next to each name is written the price of the apartment. Two-bedroom apartments always cost three million more than one-bedrooms, and the prices increase from one floor to the next. Basically, the two-bedrooms on the fifth floor are the most expensive ones in the building."

He spoke without any preamble, without any explanation, as if he knew the long wait was over. The truth was—I realized all too clearly—he couldn't care less about explaining things to my mother.

"The variations in price, however," he specified, "are not so appreciable. You, Elvira, within a week, need to let me know which tenants would like to buy their apartments, and after that, when I know who doesn't want to buy, I'll advertise that their apartments are for sale."

My mother's eyes twinkled. Perfect! At the end of the week she, the doorwoman, would step in, and upon returning the paper with the signatures, she would declare, "I will buy the Vignolas' apartment." From the restlessness of her fingers, constantly rubbing the scars on her wrists, I knew that she was tempted to reserve the apartment right away. But she refrained, afraid to voice her wish publicly for the first time, to ward off bad luck, or simply to avoid provoking the manager's brutality. She limited herself to saying, "So, have you really decided to sell Via Icaro 15?"

And he, confidentially: "Yes, Elvira, I don't want to leave behind any problems for my nephew ... buildings are nothing but trouble ... money pits ... A furnace to change, walls to reinforce, and a thousand other things ... Not to mention the estate tax ..."

My mother brought out the gold-rimmed shot glasses and poured a thimbleful of grappa for everyone. "None for me, thank you," said the engineer. The manager declined with a hand gesture—she did not say "Thank you." The grappa sat there, filling the air with its aroma.

As soon as Ingegner Spinelli and Signora Aldrovanti left, my mother grabbed the piece of paper. With her index finger she went over the names and figures over and over again, up and down, but she couldn't find what she was looking for: "Where the heck did he put the price?"

She sat down to catch her breath and then tried to pour the grappa from the glasses back into the bottle, spilling a most of it. Then she wiped down the table with a wet rag and studied the sheet of paper again.

"SIX MILLION LIRAS!"

She almost fell off her chair. Flabbergasted, she clutched the top of the stove and repeated, almost losing her voice, "SIX MILLION LIRAS! ... Where am I going to find that kind of money? What an increase! At the other buildings on Via Icaro the one-bedrooms were going for five! I don't have six million. It was all I could do to come up with four and a half ..."

"What a fool I am!" she suddenly brightened. "But of course! I'll ask for a discount from the ingegnere! A million more, a million less, what will it matter to him, with all the money he's got? And what should it matter to his heir? He won't even notice. The ingegnere would never refuse me. You heard how nice he was earlier ... Now there's a man with a heart, not like that iceberg Aldrovanti ..."

She was smiling, reassured.

"What if dad is against it?" I ventured.

She didn't lose her smile. "Your father ..." she whispered, lost in thought.

Indeed. When should she break the news to him? ... Right away or toward the end of the week, after everyone had let their intentions be known? No, best to do it right away. She had to speak with him that very night and come right out with it: "The ingegnere dropped by ..." And my father would exclaim, "The ingegnere? What did he want?" And she: "Can you guess ..." And he: "He's putting the building up for sale ..." And then? ... My father would realize that if he opposed her, she would go berserk and give him the silent treatment. And she wouldn't let up. She would only say, "At last I'm going to buy a house, too. For twenty years I've been working myself to the bone ..."

My father came home from work later than usual. He washed his hands, turned on the TV, and sat down at the table without even glancing at the newspaper. My mother let him eat in peace. Then, before serving him coffee, in a forced voice, as if she were speaking with a stranger, she said that Ingegner Spinelli had dropped by. Dad didn't lose his cool. He was too busy listening to the TV, or at least pretending to.

"Did you hear me? The landlord dropped by ..." she tried again, already worked up, standing in front of the gas stove.

"The landlord?" he echoed her mechanically. "What did he want?" He wasn't at all interested in listening to her reply. He started inveighing against Nixon: "The Americans are going to destroy us all, sooner or later. Fascists! They're not republicans! They're fascists!"

"What do you mean, 'What did he want?' Can't you figure it out?"

"What do I know? He never comes by ..." he mumbled, chewing on a tough piece of steak.

"He brought the sheet of paper with the price list ... He's selling! Do you get it? We're going to become a condominium!"

The use of the first person plural instantly distracted my father's attention from the Americans on the news.

"What you mean is *they* are going to become a condominium," he corrected her.

"What, you don't think we're as good as everyone else?" she sputtered. "We're going to buy, too, my dear, you'll see!"

"Elvira, let's not start with this again! I don't want to buy any apartment ... I've already told you a thousand times. And where do you think we're going to get the money to do it?"

"We've got the money, you know that perfectly well! I've been saving up for years. We *have* it!"

"Not on your life. I told you. NO! Not another word ..."

"We don't need a mortgage. We can pay for everything with cash!"

"And where are you going to get the money for the fees? And for the utility and phone bills?" He stared at her with hostility. "You make it sound so easy! As if it was just a question of paying for the house! What about the lawyer? Damn whoever invented them! ... Then there's the whole plumbing system that has to be repaired ... And once you start fixing things there's no end to it—painting the walls, the doors, the windows ..."

"We can paint them ourselves! I could paint a whole building if I put my mind to it ..."

"And the furniture? We don't have any furniture. It all costs money, you know! What, you don't believe me?"

"At first we'll only buy the necessities. This stove is still good ..."

My father moved from his chair to the armchair, where a tabloid magazine was waiting for him on the armrest. "Do me a favor!" he snorted, scanning the front page with an exaggerated eye movement. "I can already hear you: over here we need an end table, over there a nice sofa. And then you'll want a cabinet for all your little knickknacks and a new set of dishes and crystal glasses ... curtains for the bedroom ... an electric vacuum cleaner ..."—he shook his head while my mother struggled to swallow, as if she were before a judge with the power to sentence her to death—"We can't afford it. Why can't you understand this? Remember where we came from ... you're not born to be a signora!"

"And who said I have to be a signora? Do you think I want to spend all day doing nothing? I'll keep working. I'll start working for another family ... They'll be plenty of money to pay the bills!"

My father let her keep fantasizing, with a scornful look on his face.

He didn't know how to stop her. Then, after a deep sigh, just when it seemed he was more open to discussion, he suddenly shouted: "Mother of God, When I say no I mean no!" To emphasize the inflexibility of his reply, he stood up and pounded his fist against the wall.

All the windows in the loge started to shake, so my mother thought it best to drop the matter for the moment. But she brought it up again in bed, with renewed energy. No matter how resolved he was to dissuade her, he very quickly ran out of reasons. "What if, after we've bought it, the Vignolas don't want to leave anymore?" He was playing his last card. "What are we going to do with an occupied apartment?"

"First of all," she explained in a soothing voice, convinced that she had finally broken his resistance, "they're definitely leaving—they've always said they would. In a little while she's having a baby and they need another room for the child. They even want a second child ..."

"But at first they could keep the cradle in their room ..."

"Certainly, at first ... and in the meantime we'll be collecting the money from the rent. It'll be no loss. I could stay in the loge for another year if I knew that I had a house waiting for me ..."

My dad sighed, seemingly defeated. "Won't we have to get a lawyer to evict them? Lawyers cost an arm and a leg ..."

"Relax ... let me take care of it. Have I ever steered you wrong?"

At six o'clock she was by the stove preparing breakfast. To make sure none of the tenants got away, she opened the loge fifteen minutes early. The first person to run into her was Paolini, who always left very early, even before my father.

"Signor Paolini! Do you have a minute? The landlord is selling ..." she started to explain, almost stuttering, "and if you want to buy your apartment, well, have a look here, we'll need your signature ..."

She handed him the sheet of paper and a ballpoint pen. Paolini gave a skeptical look at the list of all the families in the complex next to a row of numbers with six zeros.

"He's selling?! ... He can be my guest. I've got to go to work ..."

"Talk to your wife ... You've got one week, if you want to buy ..."

He was already running toward the gate.

"Don't get so worked up, Elvira," my father teased her, while he was splashing aftershave on his face. "You'd think you were getting a commission!"

I didn't go to school that day.

She showed the paper to the passing tenants, while I mopped the landings, polished the brass carpet rods, and sorted the mail into the mailboxes.

In the morning, no one she approached said they were interested in buying.

"If you want," I proposed, while we were having lunch, "I can bring the sheet up to the Maestra ... Otherwise, who knows when you'll see her ..."

I missed her more and more: time passed and she hadn't come looking for me. In my ears I could still hear the last time she called out to me: "Luca . . ." I still regretted not answering her, not going straight back to her.

"Oh, alright . . ." she consented, turning red in a fit of jealousy. "But you'll never hear the end of it if . . ."

I didn't let her finish.

I climbed the stairs two at a time. When I got to her door I hesitated. Was she waiting for me? Would she rejoice the way she used to every time I came to see her unexpectedly?

She had turned into a shadow of herself, the shadow of a shadow. Her face was of a glacial pallor. Her forehead had widened. Her withered and stooped body was awash in clothes that were too big. Her dignity remained intact, but she had taken on a wounded, macabre appearance.

She appeared neither surprised nor happy to see me. Her eyes looked in another direction, and not only because she was slightly cross-eyed. Every trace of nostalgia drained from my heart. The only thing I felt was a great desire to run away.

"I came up to tell you that the landlord is selling . . ." I whispered.

She closed one eye and leaned her head toward her left shoulder. I reworded my message: the building was being put up for sale, and the tenants could buy their apartments. If she was interested in hers, she should put her signature on this piece of paper . . .

Even after my long explanation she did not emit a sound. She moved a hand in the direction of the paper, in slow motion, as if to say she didn't want to hear about it, that I should take it away. And she closed the door. Or rather, she withdrew into the shadows, like an image which, having emerged from the depths of a black sea, sinks back into it.

I was turning around to go back home when, from the other side of the wall, I heard an echo of laughter—the bitter laughter of the Maestra.

By suppertime my mother had only managed to get two signatures: the signature of Signorina Terzoli and of Signora Vezzali. There had been no sight or sound of the Vignolas. We left my father on guard duty, so to speak—since he was comfortably seated in his armchair, with his legs spread out, reading the newspaper—and went upstairs to the second floor.

Signor Vignola opened the door and immediately told us that his wife was in bed—she had started to feel some suspicious pains. He hadn't gone to the office that day out of fear that something might happen to her (which is why we hadn't seen him coming or going). My mother had no comment. During the day she had perfected the best formula and she was there to recite it.

"The landlord has decided to sell. If you are interested in buying the apartment where you live, you have to put your signature on this piece of paper as soon as possible."

I had already heard her act out the formula, with the most varied intonations, depending on the tenant, but with Vignola she threw it in his face with one breath, without personality, as if she were spitting out a cherry pit for fear of choking.

At first he twisted his face, then he repeated the words to himself, and finally, having turned them over in his head, his features relaxed into a crooked smile. In those few seconds, my mother's expression must have changed a hundred times.

"No thank you, we're not interested," he finally said. "My wife and I are looking for a larger home. This place is a hole ..."

She felt so happy she almost hugged him. But she limited herself to asking: "Do you already have an idea of when you might leave? I mean, when you would be moving ..."

"By the end of the year, we hope ..."

He provided no details. But for the moment, that would be enough for her.

The crook, to hell with him! What would it have cost him to leave everything the way it was? It was always the others who ended up paying! ... Their curses extended to his heir, the nephew. The landlord—as Signora Vezzali had established—was selling because of that spineless creature who spent all his time living the good life on the French Riviera. And with his dissolute lifestyle how long was the money going to last? ... Was he even the son of his sister? Had anyone ever seen the ingegnere with a woman by his side? As far as Dell'Uomo could tell, he'd never been married—and whatever the case, he had no children. Odd, for such a strong and healthy man ... There had always been something suspicious about his fastidious elegance, for that matter ... Not to mention he was always so rushed, so aloof, as if he had something to hide.

After a few days, malice and insults waned. Acceptance started to take hold and disgust mutated into curiosity. Now the same people had started to talk about the future more cheerfully. The building was up for sale? Good! Who was buying? Who wasn't buying? ...

Everyone wanted to know everyone else's next move, but no one dared to ask anyone else directly. And no one revealed their own intentions. As a result, everyone asked the doorwoman.

"They're going to make me crazy," my mother kept repeating, running back and forth between the intercom, the door, and the window, but in her heart she was having the time of her life, because she could see them tormenting each other and could keep them guessing with ambiguous allusions and partial—if not downright wrong—information.

The third person to sign was Mantegazza. The others, however, couldn't stop thinking and rethinking, wanting to know if their neighbor was buying—and if so, maybe they would try to buy both their own apartment and their neighbor's. And if not, then they wouldn't buy either. Or they would rail against the prices of the apartments. D'Antonio, who was the fourth person to sign, said—and he wasn't wrong—that the walls were made out of cardboard, so thin you could hear your upstairs and downstairs neighbors belching, not to mention that the pipes were old and rusty ...

By the end of the week—after the *nos* had become *yeses* and the *yeses* had become *nos* and the *nos* had gone back to being *yeses*—it was a done deal. A little because of outright antagonism, a little—but less—out of vanity, and very little out of any real desire, all the *tenants* had decided to become *owners*, which they consecrated by solemnly applying their signature to the now wrinkled price list.

The only ones who didn't want to buy were the Vignolas, the D'Antonios (he stopped by to erase his signature just a few hours after he applied it), the Casellis, and ... Miss Lynd.

My mother was waiting by the gate. She had gathered her hair behind her neck with black bobby-pins—the kind you can't see—applied lipstick, and rouged her cheeks. She was wearing a blue polka-dot Sunday suit and her one pair of high-heeled shoes. She had even put on her gold earrings. She was unrecognizable.

"Get a move on it, Chino, I have to go! . . . The spaghetti is already on your plate. I don't know what time I'll be back. It shouldn't take me too long. But the landlord's office is way the heck out there, near Piazza San Babila. It'll take me almost an hour to get there . . . Come on, sweetheart, we're in the final stretch! Today your mother is going to conclude the deal of a lifetime!"

She checked her appearance one more time in the window of a parked car.

"No, no earrings . . ." she decided, bending forward. With a little difficulty, since she wasn't used to it, she removed them from her ears and placed them in her jacket pocket. "If he sees me with my jewelry he might say, 'Do you really expect me to believe you're short of money!' But these earrings are the only memento I have from my poor mother . . . How do I look? . . . Am I or am I not a beautiful signora? . . . I hardly look like a doorwoman! Give us a kiss . . ."

She gave me a quick peck on the lips and ran toward the gate, holding her bun with her right hand. I continued watching her until she disappeared behind the hill.

I was only able to eat a couple of bites. I cleared the table and went to sit by the window. The day was magical, blue, fragrant. The cat was making its rounds of the courtyard. Lately it had taken to walking with difficulty, lazy and disoriented. The birds flitted nearby, un-afraid—and she made no attempt to catch them.

Almost three hours had passed when I recognized her dark out-line in the distance. She walked slowly through the clouds of dust, looking like she had just returned from war. Her hair had mostly come undone—long locks tumbled down her neck and over her pale forehead. Not a trace of makeup or blush remained.

She didn't want to speak. She undressed, splashed some water un-der her armpits, then put on the clothes she normally wore during working hours. She gathered up my father's overalls, which had been in the pile behind the bedroom door, placed them on the armchair, opened up the ironing board, plugged in the iron, and started iron-ing. Moistened by steam, the fabric released the greasy smell of the factory.

I took the leftover spaghetti and went down to the space beneath the stairs. The cat arrived a little later with an appreciative meow and stuck her face into the saucer. I waited for her to finish eating.

When I got back home, my mother was ironing another pair of overalls. "I'm not running some kind of a white sale," she recited in her usual voice, without interrupting her ironing. She worked art-fully. The iron guided her hand rather than the other way around. The tip was inserted firmly into the corners, stopping at exactly the right moment, as if it had a mind of its own. The iron glided over the fabric—not a single motion was wasted—racing headlong, slalom-ing, zigzagging, speeding up and slowing down as needed. Using the most suitable pressure, she ironed out every wrinkle.

"That's what he said to me: 'I'm not running some kind of a white sale.' Get it? Not another word. No, wait—one more thing he told me: 'Where do you want to go, Elvira? The condominium needs someone like you' ... Oh, dear Chino, no discounts ... He left me speechless ... Who would've expected it? It took him a minute to send me packing. He got right to the point. 'I'm not running some kind of a white sale.' ... But he kept me waiting for an hour ... What does he care if I can't buy the house? ... I was so wrong about him ... I thought he was refined, I believed—what a fool I am!—that he admired me, and instead he's just like Aldrovanti. Actually he's worse. At least she doesn't try to sweet-talk you with a lot of hogwash ..."

The dream was over. The fantasies were over. The perennial waiting was over. Over, over, over ... My mother could forget about the Vignolas' house; forget about the curtains; forget about the new sofa bed for me. A doorwoman she was and a doorwoman she would remain ...

"Hey, enough of that?" she yelled at me. "Stop looking at me. Don't you have homework to do?"

I retreated to the bedroom and started to cry, huddled up behind the bed, in the same place that I had cried over the Maestra.

I went back to my mother, picked up the pressed and folded overalls, and placed them in the armoire. From then on I would be the most helpful son in the world.

"Can I make you a coffee, mother?"

Through the window she was looking at the clock in the lobby. It was late for coffee.

"Sure, why not," she said after a moment's hesitation.

She no longer had the same long face as before. In her eyes a new light was shining. She smiled at me.

"What are you thinking?" I asked while handing her the cup.

She took a sip.

"Ah, you really know how to make a good coffee! ... What am I thinking? I'm thinking that I'll get that money from Gemma. I find it hard to believe that she wouldn't have a million to lend me ... Alfio makes a decent salary from the railways, and when it's not his shift, he earns something on the side as a house painter."

Two minutes later Gemma arrived.

"Well?" she asked impatiently.

My mother waited until she was seated.

"I'm about to buy!"

Gemma batted her eyelashes.

"Buy what?"

"What do you mean, 'Buy what?' . . . the Vignolas' apartment . . ."

"Oh! . . ."

She wasn't showing any of the joy we expected—she didn't even bother to smile.

"Who knows, maybe one day we . . ." she sighed. "But we're just starting out. You, Elvira have been working yourself to the bone for half a century! Chino is grown up now and can help you to pay the mortgage and the expenses, which add up. Set him up as an apprentice to a plumber or mechanic—he'll bring home a nice paycheck! Plumbers and mechanics, now those guys make serious money, those sons of bitches!—and so do cooks!"

I listened, holding my breath.

Adept at playing her cards right, even in the most stressful situations, my mother didn't say a word about my future. "Gemma, also on Paride's behalf, I want to ask a big favor of you and your husband. A huge favor . . . If I didn't need to, I wouldn't have the courage to ask . . . Paride doesn't want to hear any talk about mortgages. We're buying in cash. *We have to!* But I don't have the full amount. The one-bedroom costs six rather than five million. I don't know why, but in the end the landlord raised the price. Take it or leave it, he said—and if I don't take it this time, it'll be over. When am I going to get another opportunity like this? I've been saving my whole life. I'm almost there. But I'm short one million damn liras, and he refused to give me any kind of discount . . . Could you find it in your heart to lend me the money? Of course I'd lend it to you without a second thought! And I could pay you back within a year, I swear, with interest. You know how good I am at finding work and saving. I'm not like the *signore* at the building next door . . . Who knows where they got the money. If only I could wait another year . . . but I have to let him know by the day after to-morrow. If I don't, someone else is going to buy the Vignolas' place. I think the seamstress, that awful Signora Bortolon, has already got her eyes on it. And I would lose out. *Lose out! . . .*"

Gemma touched her arm. She wanted it to seem like an affectionate gesture, but it wasn't. "If you miss this chance there'll always be another. Maybe closer to downtown. Here we're out in the boondocks . . ."

My mother jumped as if her friend had given her an electric shock. "But here houses cost less, don't you understand? . . ." She rubbed her scars. "And I've become fond of Via Icaro. I don't want to leave. The only thing I want is to have my own house. To close the door and not to have to see or hear anyone. Can you lend me that million? Please. In a year I'll pay you back with all the interest . . ."

She wouldn't even consider the idea of abandoning Via Icaro, that godforsaken road out in the sticks. If she was going to become a homeowner, it had to be here. Here, where they had humiliated her, where they had treated her like a servant. So only *here* could her claim to freedom become a form of revenge.

"I'll have to speak with Alfio . . ." Gemma hesitated, "he's the one that keeps the books in the family . . . I don't know if we have a million. I really don't know . . . You were right when you wondered how the signore get their money! But we're not like that. Alfio works himself to death. And is it worth it in the end?"

My mother took her hands. "So you'll talk to him tonight? Promise?"

Another long wait had begun, even harder than the others: all of a sudden our entire future, our happiness, depended on Gemma.

Still ignoring the situation, my father, at supper, told us the plot of the film *The Seduction of Mimi*, down to the smallest details. Then he started criticizing Bertolucci. Brando's monologue to his dead wife in *The Last Tango* was a joke ... and so were the rape scene, the mumbled sentences, the finger in the ass—ridiculous! ... And *The Canterbury Tales* of Pasolini? Even worse. The work of a pervert. Dicks everywhere you looked ...

He did all the talking. My mother and I kept looking in the direction of the telephone.

"Would you mind telling me what the hell is wrong with you two tonight?" he yelled, exasperated.

Her nerves were on edge and she turned around in a flash.

"Nothing," she seethed, "what do you think is wrong?"

"You're a couple of bores," he said, the most offensive thing he could come up with.

By the following morning Gemma still hadn't given her answer. I went back to school and my mother kept waiting. She didn't dare telephone, fearing she would irritate her friend. But the clock was ticking. There was only one day left.

At two-thirty, with my encouragement, she decided to call. Her husband picked up. He said that Gemma had gone to Carmen's for a coffee.

We waited another hour. My mother tried again. Luckily Gemma was back.

"Did you talk to Alfio?" she asked, getting right to the point. "You haven't?... But Gemma, I told you I had to give my answer now—tomorrow, or I'll lose the apartment! For heaven's sake, put yourself in my shoes! ... Listen, let's forget about it ..."

She slammed the phone down, furious, and still wearing her clogs she hurried out the door.

"Where are you going?" I shouted at her from the window.

"To Carmen's!"

She came back a few minutes later, all red in the face and sweating.

"I came so close to slapping her across the face. What a fool I am! Of all people to ask for a favor! In my opinion they're in the cahoots. Fine friends they are ... and who knows what they're going to say behind my back now!"

She got back on the phone.

"Gemma, I apologize for what I said earlier. I'm a bundle of nerves, try to understand. I've been waiting for this moment for years. So can you please let me know *by tonight*, don't forget!" And she added, a second before hanging up, "Thanks also on Paride's behalf."

A little before seven the telephone rang. My mother was about to drain the pasta. She dropped everything in the sink—pasta, boiling water, kettle—and ran to answer it. The only thing we heard her say was, "I see." She hung up the phone, went back to the sink, and started retrieving the macaroni.

We sat down to the table. Her eyes had become as big as two lakes. She looked at me and in her gaze I saw a last heroic glimmer of determination. She waited for me to close and lock the front door. My father sat down in the armchair to watch television—but she turned it off. Paying no heed to his protests, she said with no ifs, ands, or buts, that it would cost six million to buy the house: six, not five.

He had a bemused expression, then he jumped to his feet. With a sweep of the hand he knocked all the knickknacks off the fold-out bed and started kicking the chairs.

"You thought you were going to fuck me over?" he gasped, as if he were about to cough, circling her like a maniac. "Me? For Christ's sake ..."

"Shut up! Do you want the whole building to hear you? Do you want us to become a laughing stock?"

He kept shaking his head and waving his arms around.

"Where did you think you were going to find the money, huh? Did you even think about what you were doing? DID YOU EVEN THINK ABOUT WHAT YOU WERE DOING? You wanted to ruin me! That's what you wanted! And like an idiot I followed you! Where did you think you were going to get the money—growing on trees?"

With her back against the wall, my mother finally uttered the word that she had been struggling to avoid: "We could always apply for a mortgage. What's wrong with that? Not everyone buys with cash on the barrel. Not even Signora Dell'Uomo, I hear, who is hardly hurting for money. For that matter she doesn't even have children to take care of ..."

At the sound of the word "mortgage" my father's face turned to ash.

"Mortgages are the ruin of the world," he hollered at the top of his lungs. "What the fuck do I have to say to make you understand?"

He panted, placing his hand over his chest. We thought he was having a heart attack. My mother helped him sit in the armchair, fanned his face with her hand, and asked him fearfully whether she should call the doctor.

He stood up in a sweat and very slowly made his way to the bed-room.

I spent the night trying to overhear any words that might've come from their room. But not a word was said. The only thing I could hear was the ticking of the alarm clock.

More than anything, even more than defeat, she was oppressed by the thought that she had become an object of ridicule. She had brought universal disdain on herself: everyone knew of her failure and relished it. Now she saw the curled lips in their customary greetings as an affront or even a reprimand.

"They're all laughing in my face! And they're right! I couldn't even buy my own house! They're right to laugh! Ha-ha-ha! Very funny!"

And she wept like a fountain, her hands balled into fists, her mouth drooling uncontrollably.

She stopped speaking to my father. What was left to say? Nothing. Instead of words, gasps and sobs came out of her mouth. She couldn't breathe. Out of the blue she would drop whatever she was doing and run to the window for air. Every day she became more listless—she wasted away.

Disappointment had aged her visibly and she suddenly looked ten years older. "What's wrong, Elvira?" the signore would ask. "Are you tired?" So as not to give them any satisfaction, she would reply, "What do I have to be tired about? Elvira is never tired! She's like a mule!"

Even my father asked her what was wrong, but she refused to answer him.

She would go out without telling me. She'd go to sit on a bench in the garden, under the willow tree, and stay there for fifteen minutes at a time. When people asked for her, I had to run and call her, and I'd find her motionless, in a daze. "Momma, they're looking for you," I would whisper, trying not to startle her. Not even the name "Aldrovanti" was enough to shake her out of it—the same name that had struck the fear of God into her a few days earlier now left her completely indifferent. "Tell her I'll call back ..." she would reply nonchalantly.

One day I ran almost all the way to the streetcar stop to get her. She'd decided to go to the Rinascente department store downtown to spend five hundred thousand liras in a single shot. What did she need the money for anymore? In the meantime, with no one keeping watch at the door, a couple of Jehovah's Witnesses had snuck up the stairs. But Terzoli stopped them immediately, threatening to call the police. "What a bunch of creeps!" she told my mother. "They'd rather let a child die than give it a blood transfusion! We'd better not let management find out about these little visits ..." My mother didn't bat an eye. She didn't give a damn about appearing infallible anymore. Nor was she worried about criticism, complaints, and threatening insinuations.

She had lost all desire to work. She'd also lost the physical strength she needed to clean so many floors. What she used to finish in a morning now took her a whole week. The bucket and the scrub-brush would be left forgotten in the lobby for days on end.

I was mad at my father—he had been unfair and selfish. But he needed some sympathy, too. He was waiting for a sign of reconciliation from her, a sign that never came. During supper he would stare at her, smile at her, studying her movements lovingly, convinced that the simple insistence of his gaze would induce her to give in. But nothing. She ignored him with a demented obstinacy, made even more monstrous in that it conveyed no anger.

Now the building was in the hands of twenty owners.

All of them adopted an insufferable haughtiness, morning, noon, and night. Even I could feel it. They would walk by the loge with a sneer, giving long, smug looks, as if to say, "Did you hear? I'm an owner. I'M AN OWNER!"

Many of them stopped saying hello, and the signore started to expect the most absurd things from the doorwoman—like sweeping their doormats or polishing their doors. They all wanted an impeccable, *refined* building, and each of them, as an owner, felt they had the right to demand whatever they pleased, no matter how outrageous, and had no respect for either the doorwoman or their neighbors. Some didn't even bother to throw their garbage bags down the chute, leaving their trash sitting on the landing.

Misbehavior doubled, as did complaints and fights. Rovigo and Paolini, old buddies, came to blows over a parking spot, even though in front of the apartment complex there were miles of empty land. Tension between the soccer fans was exacerbated, and on the balconies—despite a strict prohibition by the management—the flags of Milan's rival clubs started to appear.

Dell'Uomo, who hadn't been able to have children, told Vezzali that she had only been able to give birth after two miscarriages. Mortally offended, Vezzali spread the word that Dell'Uomo did indeed have a son, but she kept him hidden at the Asylum for the Disabled, with the armless and legless creatures.

An endless circuit of gossip brought to light the true ages of the various signore. It became known that Terzoli, for example, was only four years younger than my father. But she looked the same age as Mantegazza.

My mother didn't want to hear another word about letting the kittens loose in the field. This year we had to kill them, and quickly, before they strayed into the courtyard—otherwise we'd never hear the end of it from the building manager.

I went downstairs to look for them in the basement, but no luck.

Rita had noticed that the cat, after it licked the plate of leftovers, would run behind the building. We went looking for her there, where no one dared to venture because of the loose wall tiles, and found her at the foot of the magnolia tree.

"Here, kitty, kitty. Show me and Chino where you hid your little babies," Rita sweet-talked her. "Take us to them . . . Come on!"

The cat, as if enchanted by the sound of the girl's voice, turned to gaze at the wall of ivy marking the end of the garden.

I brushed aside the leaves and saw them.

The cat picked them up one by one in her mouth—there were six— and put them in a row. Then she lay down on her side to nurse them.

With the same naturalness as the animal who had stretched out to nurse her newborns, Rita pulled up her T-shirt.

"Do you want to touch them?" she asked me. "If you like, I'll let you suckle them, like a kitty."

She grabbed my hand and placed it over her breast. Her nipples were hard.

"Now we're engaged," she announced.

At sunset, after using a bowl of milk to entice the cat to go down to the cellar, I led my mother to the secret lair. The kittens were awake and mewling softly, one after the other. My mother picked them up with one hand, two at a time, and stuffed them into a plastic bag from the supermarket.

"What're you looking at?" she scolded me. "If I start feeling sorry for cats, then I'm really pathetic. Does anyone ever feel sorry for me?"

She tied the bag shut with a tight knot and slammed it hard against the corner of the building. One, two, three, four times, until the translucent white of the plastic bag had turned ruby red.

To keep the cat from recognizing the smell, we buried the bodies under three feet of garbage.

An unknown man appeared at the window. He was bald, his red cheeks riddled with purple veins, and wearing winter clothing.

"I'm Baioni," he introduced himself. "May I speak with the doorwoman?"

Hearing his voice, my mother rose from the bed and came out to see.

"And who might you be?"

Her eyes were swollen with sleep and her hair was glued to the nape of her neck.

Once she would have corrected him, to say that she was the *custodian*. But not anymore: now she was indifferent to everything, even to things that used to infuriate her.

To identify himself, the unknown man lifted a leather suitcase up to the window. She opened it. This was also new: when had she ever, before the sale of the building, allowed a traveling salesman to come in? Exposing herself to the risk of being attacked? Neglecting her errands, not to mention her personal security and the general order of the building? But there was something about Signor Baioni that inspired trust. He had gentle manners and a kind face, like a friar. My mother unlocked the door and invited him to follow her into her room.

Within a few seconds the large double-bed had turned into a jewelry display case. I had never seen so much gold before. I was bedazzled. My mother, instead, feigned perfect equanimity. Among the many precious items, she claimed not a single one was any good. The salesman raised his index finger to implore her to be patient. From an inside pocket of his heavy checked coat he fished out a sachet.

"Don't even bother opening it," she barked. "I've always hated colored gemstones ..."

"Your wish is my command!" Baioni said, like an obsequious waiter. "And emeralds do get scratched so easily ... You're right. For a woman like you, only diamonds will do! I should have realized immediately ... So here you are, Signora ..."

"*Signora* Elvira," she quickly interjected, flattered.

Baioni stuck his hand into another secret pocket and extracted a small doeskin sachet.

"Inside you'll find the ring that's perfect for *you*."

With a jubilant expression he emptied the contents of the sachet into the center of the satin bedspread: a shower of jewels.

My mother tried on the rings, one at a time. He proposed the earrings, too. No, not the earrings. That would be too much.

"As you wish, Signora Elvira."

My mother studied the ring that she'd slid onto the middle finger of her left hand.

"My hands are all wrong for diamonds"—she began to pity herself—"look at them: dry, chapped ... you can't imagine how much work they've done ... and all for what?"

"There is a perfect ring for every woman," declared Baioni, a true salesman. "The hard part is to find it ... but you clearly have, Signora Elvira. An excellent choice: fourteen little diamonds and a larger central diamond in the middle ... it would be the envy of any woman ... See how nice it looks on you! With a ring like this on your finger, who'd notice how dry your skin is?"

"And how much would it cost?"

Baioni took out his price sheet.

"Six hundred thousand."

She laughed in his face. It was a tenth of the cost of the house she had wanted to buy!

"Signora Elvira, let me explain," Baioni continued passionately. "A diamond is no ordinary gemstone. It's much much more. Its value will increase! A diamond is a gift that will last a lifetime . . ."

She was unimpressed by his palaver.

"How much lower can you go?"

Baioni took a deep breath.

"I'll give it to you for five hundred, because it's your first purchase, your first diamond. An excellent price—but don't tell anyone! They'd never believe you . . . you can pay me fifty a month. It's a bargain. And it also comes with a warranty . . ."

She bit her lip. She held her hand out and brought it close. She tilted her head back, first to one side, then to the other.

"Do you like it?" she asked me.

I said I did, reminiscing about Miss Lynd's diamonds, which were ever bigger and shinier.

"The boy knows what he's talking about," Baioni smiled, while placing the other jewels back in the doeskin sachets and the little envelopes. "And you'll find that even your husband will see you in an entirely new light . . ."

My mother opened the armoire, fished out the steel box, and removed two one-hundred-lira bills. Baioni took them, and signed the receipt.

"So we'll see each other next month then . . . Ah, and do you think in the building there might be other women who . . ."

"Heavens no!" my mother stopped him. "I have strict orders not to let anyone upstairs, no Jehovah's Witnesses, no Avon ladies, and no jewelry salesmen! . . . Besides, you're not going to find anyone who deserves diamonds here . . . In here they're all petty and cheap. They think they're grand but true nobility is not what you see on the outside—it's what's on the inside that counts. Don't get me started! Do you know what I think? I don't give a damn about the lowlifes who live here. They can all go to hell. For ten years now I've been kind to everybody. Enough already. From now on I'm ignoring them. They tell me: 'Elvira, next time please remember to polish my door.' And I say: 'Of course.' But next time I won't even mop the landing. Why should I care? Do they care about me? Worthless bums ..."

Baioni was taken aback by her sudden outburst. Speechless, he made a slight bow and went on his way.

My mother sat down and studied the ring on her finger. Her face was burning. Like a remorseful thief, incapable of determining whether she had stolen a precious object or pure junk, she wondered what she had gotten herself into. What if the diamonds were fake? She'd been such an idiot! Giving her money to a complete stranger! The thought that Baioni would be coming by next month for the second installment reassured her—but what if he didn't come back? What a fool she'd been to be cheated like that! She, who knew that the world was filled with con artists!

Fearing that my father would see it, she kept the ring hidden in the steel box. When he was away, she would take it, rub it with dishwashing liquid, and then study it carefully under a lamp. For her the ring could never be too shiny. "Look at it!" she would command me. When she would ask me, "What do you think?" there was no point in answering, "It's beautiful," because something had been gnawing at her ever since that damn Baioni had dropped by. If it weren't for the two hundred liras it had cost her, she would have thrown it in the trash.

Saturday arrived. My father was getting ready to go to the movies. She was rinsing the dishes, her brow more furrowed than usual. She suddenly turned off the faucet and yanked off her apron.

"Get dressed," she ordered me, "we're going downtown ..."

"What's going on?" protested my father, who had almost finished combing his hair. "I'm about to go out ..."

"Chino," she replied while she was slipping on her shoes, "tell your father that it's our turn to go out today. Every now and then he can give up something, too. The movies will still be there tomorrow ... Lets go!"

The streetcar left us in Piazza Cordusio, where my mother had gone on walks a few times as a young woman, back when she was working for the doctor.

"Here we are," she sighed in front of a jewelry shop.

"Can I help you?" asked the owner without much conviction.

"Well, to be honest," my mother stammered, "I didn't come here to buy anything. I only wanted, if possible, to get an estimate on this ring ..."

She removed it from her jacket pocket and let it fall into the woman's outstretched hand.

"Where did you buy it?" the jeweler asked while she was examining it under the lens.

In the grip of panic, my mother told her she had found it on the street.

"It's a nice ring. The stones aren't the greatest, but they're pure. It's probably worth about seven hundred liras. If you want, I'll buy it from you. I can pay you right away ..."

My mother grabbed me by the arm.

"No thank you," she whispered. "Maybe someday, if I'm ever having difficulties ..."

She took the ring back and dragged me out of the store. A few steps later she burst into tears, in the midst of the crowd. Not only was the ring authentic, but it was worth a lot more than it had cost her! Poor Baioni! She had been so unfair to ever doubt him!

On a wave of enthusiasm, she dragged me to the Rinascente department store—the moral sewer of the city, according to my father—where she bought me a pair of brand-name jeans and treated me to a Coke at the café on the top floor. For herself she ordered an espresso and asked the waiter for a cigarette.

As we walked across the Piazza del Duomo I told her what I remembered about the history of the cathedral, pointing up to the gold statue of the Madonna suspended in the Milanese sky. She started to sing "O mia bela Madunina," but stopped after the first words. For a second we remembered the old lady's visit.

"Is it really pure gold?" she asked me incredulously. Then, she sighed: "If only I could've had just the head..."

It was time to let the rest of the building know about the diamond—then they would stop thinking that the doorwoman hadn't bought an apartment because she was short of money. They had to understand once and for all that she hadn't bought one *because she didn't want to live in that building* . . .

She invited the seamstress down for a cup of coffee: if you wanted a secret to get out as quickly as possible, who better to start with?

Nowadays the seamstress was acting like a grand capitalist. Indeed, she was the only one who had bought two apartments, her own and the one next door, the Vignolas' one-bedroom . . . She told us that in a year she'd knock down the wall, turning it into a five-room apartment. With two bathrooms! And four balconies! Two attics! And two front doors! She would have the biggest place on the block!

"We also have plenty of money," my mother said, when the seamstress finally stopped long enough to take a breath. "But there were no more two-bedrooms left, so what was I supposed to buy? A one-bedroom? Where would we put the boy? The day we leave Via Icaro, we're going to get a house with at least two-bedrooms. Chino can't keep going without his own room. Especially now that he's attending the Classical Lyceum . . ."

"If you move," the seamstress said, "you're gonna have bills to pay . . ."

"Signora Bortolon," my mother reassured her, "it'll take a lot more than an electric bill to ruin us! We've got so much money squirreled away that we don't know what to do with it . . . You know just the other day, on a whim—it's not like I needed it!—I bought myself the diamond ..."

That's how she said it, *the* diamond, the way she said *the* Classical Lyceum, like the Maestra.

The seamstress's face turned bright red.

"You got yourself the *diamond*!"

And my mother: "A setting of fourteen little stones with a big rock in the middle ..."

Letting her envy get the better of her, the seamstress shrieked: "You're not scared someone's gonna steal it?"

And my mother, growing more aloof by the minute: "What can I say? It is what it is. In the meantime, I'll keep it well hidden. Oh, and please, don't breathe a word to anyone, I know I can trust you."

The seamstress was shaking with the urge to see the diamond, but she didn't want to stoop to asking.

"What good's a diamond if you're scared someone's gonna steal it all the time? It's like you didn't even have it."

"There you're wrong, my dear Signora Bortolon! There's a big difference between having the diamond and not having it! I look at it, every now and then I try it on. I didn't buy it to show off ... the diamond is personal ... if you could only see how shiny it is!"

"So show me the damn diamond already!"

With magnanimous reserve, as if she were granting an exclusive privilege, my mother invited the seamstress to follow her into the bedroom. She reached to the back of the armoire, rummaged through the winter clothes, and after a minute emerged somewhat ruffled, wearing her trophy.

"Ooooh, how pretty," the seamstress murmured, and immediately followed in a higher-pitched tone, "Give it here so I can try it on."

My mother removed the ring and handed it to her.

"It really is pretty . . ." she concluded, after regaining her sour expression. "But what good is a ring like that? I like simple things . . ."

Within two days, all of 15 Via Icaro knew that the doorwoman had bought a diamond. *The* diamond! Dell'Uomo tried to spread the rumor that we had won the lottery. But it didn't take long for everyone to realize that, if that were the case, we wouldn't still be living there.

For my Italian finals I decided to write about freedom. While I was filling the exam sheet with words, I thought about my mother, who'd never had a taste of freedom. I thought about what I had learned from Miss Lynd: that the Italians didn't know freedom because they'd almost always been dominated. I compared them to the Russians. Like the Russians, Italians were inclined to entrust everything to a leader, whether a king, dictator, or pope—anyone who knew how to raise his voice and promise happiness for the future. I wrote that Italians didn't understand the concept of the present, at least not as well as other nations, for example the French. Italians postpone everything until tomorrow, and the next day they do the same thing, infinitely, and meanwhile they make do and try to manage with what they have. They wouldn't know what to do with real freedom because it would require hard work, dedication, constant vigilance—and Italians are lazy, a little selfish, and concerned only with themselves and their families. They don't care too much about their rights: they would rather break the law than fight to protect what was owed to them.

I wrote how true freedom gets attacked over nothing. True freedom cannot be partial, it can only be perfect. All it takes is one person, just one single member of our government, to misbehave—to disrespect the people—for freedom to become a travesty, a puppet that can be manipulated at will. I quoted a sentence by Gandhi that the Maestra had taught me: "No tyrant can govern without the active support of the people," because when there is a dictator, freedom is trampled by everyone, not just the dictator. I wrote about South Africa, Palestine, Italian colonialism . . .

At my oral exam Signorina Salma took me to task.

"Where did this boy get all these crazy ideas?" she asked her colleagues indignantly. "You wouldn't believe the idiocies he wrote about Italian colonialism! Well he didn't hear them from me! We helped the countries we colonized—and that's the truth! We were much—and I mean *much*—better than the English! And comparing us to the Russians! We Italians aren't communists!"

She started in on a passionate defense of the greatness of the Italian people. She continued with a speech about the beauty of patriotism, the sweetness of our language, which forces us to turn around when we hear it echoed in a foreign country, prompting us to search for an unknown fellow Italian, unknown but not *foreign*, like the time that she, in Paris, during her honeymoon, overheard, in the midst of a crowd, a short sentence uttered in Italian—and she couldn't identify where it had come from. But for the rest of the day the sound stayed with her, or rather *in* her, as if it had slipped under her skin, making that foreign city feel less foreign, where no one knew her, and where they ate the most absurd things, like pasta as a side dish instead of a first course! ...

The geography teacher, Signora Marelli, who'd never hidden her sympathies for neo-fascism, said seraphically, "Don't get so worked up, Salma. Ideas come and ideas go, but the good ones always stay!" And to me, before she started in with her questions on that year's curriculum: "Graziosi, just for the sake of it, how does your father vote?"

"That will be enough," ruled Barro, the technical applications teacher, barely concealing his anger. "The boy wrote what he thinks. What are we going to do, put him on trial? Is the composition well written? It is? So we're going to pass him, and with a good grade. For my part I don't have to ask him anything. And he's right, Italian colonialism was shameful."

I passed Italian, Latin, and English with distinction, and I did well in all the other subjects, too. I received compliments from the whole exam committee, including, at the end, Signorina Salma. But she gave me a strange look, as if she suddenly realized that she had been harboring a viper in her classroom for the past three years.

Caselli, in a bathrobe, jittery as a junebug, kept repeating that she had only seen her in mid-air.

"So then tell me," the police commissioner pressed on with the patience of a bureaucrat, "what did you see, in the exact order ..."

And it was the same story.

"If I had seen her perched on the balcony I would have said something to her," Caselli tried to justify herself. "I was smoking a cigarette. I couldn't sleep ... at five o'clock in the morning it was already so hot I couldn't breathe."

My mother was crying. She had been the first person to go down to the courtyard, after Caselli called her on the intercom.

"Poor Maestra!" she kept repeating.

I had made it just in time to notice, through the window blinds, the stretcher-bearers draping a sheet over the corpse and lifting it into the ambulance.

After Caselli came Terzoli, Miss Lynd's neighbor. She hadn't heard anything in particular, she said. Or rather yes, she did, the sound of the toilet being flushed, repeatedly. That's what had woken her up. The sound of water got on her nerves. Miss Lynd had never made so much noise at night. She was one of the quietest people she had ever met. Yes, of course, she was a little crazy, greeting everyone with strange, incomprehensible words and never confiding in anyone—if only all neighbors were like her!

"You couldn't tell whether she had any company?" the commissioner asked.

"I don't think so."

"Another voice ..."

"Do you mean someone pushed her?" the spinster was already letting her imagination run wild. "Good God! Why? ... you don't think it was the gypsies, do you?"

"Signora, do you live with someone?"

"No, I'm single," she replied, with her head held high.

"Thanks, you can go back home now ..."

Disappointed that she hadn't been questioned more at length, she tightened the belt of her bathrobe and took the elevator.

My mother poured the officer a cup of coffee.

"What about all that blood?" she wondered. "We can't leave a stain like that where everyone passes by. Who knows how long before someone removes it. And it'll take a lot more than ten bucketfuls of water. What do you think—you, an expert in these things?"

He said she would need ammonia.

"So do you think she was murdered?" my mother suggested.

"To your knowledge did Miss Lynd suffer from nerves? Was she ill? I mean, do you have any reason to believe she didn't want to live anymore? ... A reason to kill herself? ... Why does everyone say she was crazy?"

"They're the ones who are crazy!" my mother corrected him. "Miss Lynd was a great lady, a real signora ... but if she was ill—I wouldn't know ..."

Now it was my turn.

I told him that Miss Lynd had taught me English, that she used to give me snacks, that she knew a lot of things ...

"OK, that will do ..." the policeman cut me short.

The next morning a letter arrived for me. It was postmarked five days earlier. Shaking, I folded the envelope in two and hid it in my pants pocket. I finished separating the rest of the mail, made three signs of the cross, and began to read:

My dear Luca,

I'm leaving. I was lucky to meet you. Thanks to you I was able to fool myself into thinking I had rediscovered my youth. I hope you will continue on your own what we started together. You definitely have the energy and the conviction. You once asked me what had happened to my English dictionary. When I told you that I had grown tired of working on it, I was lying. The truth is I had stopped believing in the possibility of giving precise meanings to words. That's why I abandoned it. What a disaster! My whole life had been spent defining things. And all of a sudden … something in me stopped working, or maybe it finally started working properly. Who knows? I'd been so unhappy since the day my dictionary died. But you made me want to give it another try. Our lessons made it suddenly seem possible again. I could pretend that everything had a meaning and a purpose. To define! But it doesn't—it isn't like that. At least not for me. I wanted to instill in you a confidence that had forsaken me a long time ago. Please don't accuse me of inconsistency or hypocrisy. With you I started to believe in language again. Or rather, I fooled myself into thinking I had started to believe again. But that wasn't the case … Now all I see are the lies inside me. And when I remember what I used to be like as a girl! The faith I had in meanings, which I collected, just the way you do in your notebooks! Keep them close to you, these notebooks! And when, perhaps, you are tempted by doubts, take them out, reread them, don't hide them the way I hid my own work.

Farewell,

Amelia

IV

M y mother came looking for me under the wisteria tree.
"Miss Lynd had a son!"

She was huffing and puffing as if she'd gone up and down the staircase ten times.

My Latin book fell down off my knees and the letter from the Maestra, which I kept hidden between the pages, slipped out of the book and onto the gravel. Luckily my mother didn't notice. I bent down to pick it up and hide it again.

"Did you hear? A son! He just called on the telephone. He's coming by this afternoon. He's the one who bought her apartment! His name is Ippolito Foschi! . . . Ippolito . . . What the heck kind of name is that? . . . She certainly was a strange one, that Lynd! Are you sure she never told you anything about him?"

He was tall and thin, with his mother's fine features—and while in her they hinted at the remnants of a former beauty, in him they revealed a protracted, indelible adolescence. He, too, smiled with a certain ease. Yes, he did look a lot like her. But there was also something in him of the Foschi who had given him his surname. I strained to recognize that other part. I felt as if I could identify it in the narrowing of his jaw, the quivering of his wide nostrils, the sudden iciness of his stare. (While she, even when she was railing against the world, conserved a warm light in her eyes.) Before him I felt as if I were in the presence of a Christ-like figure, in whom I had to distinguish between the godly and the human parts: the father and the mother.

Ippolito Foschi, the secret son, was the living, tangible symbol

of the great mystery hidden in the life of Maestra Lynd. I looked
at him with religious awe, as if the dead woman had decided to be
reincarnated through him, to give me the extreme proof of her unimaginable, unquantifiable power, subjugating me, once and for all,
to her dominion.

"Miss Lynd was such a good woman, such a civil woman ..." my
mother said to cheer him up.

"Really? I'm pleased to hear it ..." he replied absently.

"She was the one who caused me the least amount of trouble ..."

"Well, she didn't cause me much trouble, either, to tell you the
truth. We hadn't seen each other for twenty years."

My mother and I were paralyzed with dismay. On her creased
forehead I could read a host of questions that were not transfigured
into words. Foschi's manner didn't encourage questions or com-
ments.

The three of us went up to the fifth floor. He only stayed for ten
minutes.

My mother reported that he had looked around the apartment
incuriously, gone to the balcony, and stuck his head out, without
uttering a word or shedding a tear the whole time.

"He must be in shock, poor thing! We should put ourselves in his
shoes ..."

Signora Dell'Uomo, in her role as the condominium representative, descended the stairs to interrogate the doorwoman. My mother cut her no slack, limiting herself to saying that the Professor—that's the title she came up with—was a *very proper* person.

"Very *smiley*," Signora Dell'Uomo specified, "a little too smiley, wouldn't you say? As if the tragedy had nothing to do with him ... what does he say about his mother? I mean, she fell from the fifth floor. I'm sure she had her reasons!"

"The Professor is very reserved. Besides, why should he have to say anything? It was a tragedy. The time for words is over. What's needed now is silence ..."

"Of course, of course ... but I think it's absurd that the son had no comment about the *suicide* of his mother!"—she shuddered as she said the word—"What I mean is that she died right before our eyes. In the courtyard there's a bloodstain that will disappear god knows when. We have a right to know, don't we? If you ask me she had something weighing on her conscience ... There was no sight or sound of him until yesterday. Why is it that he's only now making an appearance? Where has he been till now? What kind of a son is he!"

Most of the building showed up at the Maestra's funeral. At the mortuary in the Niguarda Hospital there were neither priests nor flowers, except a spindly wreath from the condominium. The coffin was closed, since there was so little left to see of Amelia Lynd.

The seamstress offered to accompany him to the cemetery, but the Professor refused: the coffin was going straight to the crematorium.

The malice began the second he got into the car. They had something to say about everything: there was no mass, the coffin was cheap, the body was cremated! What they disapproved of most of all was his composure. He didn't shed a tear! Scandalous!

For days and days my mother repeated, as the commissioner himself had asserted, that the death of Miss Lynd had been an accident of the kind that happens to the elderly. She couldn't sleep, she got up to get a breath of fresh air on the balcony, she lost her balance ...

But they weren't satisfied with this version of the incident. It failed to explain too many things. For example, why didn't the Professor want a religious funeral for his mother? "Nowadays the church also accepts suicides, if indeed it was suicide," Terzoli observed. And Vezzali, "Of course he shipped the body straight to the oven: what better way to get rid of the proof than a nice bonfire? ..." And why hadn't he wept? Why did he have nothing to say there, in front of the mortuary? Why didn't he bother to thank the attendees and apologize? And those smiles? Who did he think he was fooling? And above all, if Lynd was washing the windows, why didn't the police find a damp cloth or Windex? Not to mention there was plenty of space between the windows and the railings of the balcony. The Maestra would've needed to take a flying leap, which was impossible for a woman of her age.

The summer smothered all this malice beneath its muggy dome. Now the hens had something else to keep their minds occupied. They complained that they were broke, although they were still unwilling to give up their vacations. Some were going to the seaside, some to the mountains, others to the countryside. The doorwoman had better keep an eye on their property! They even expected her, in their absence, to inspect—around the clock, on a daily basis—every lock, floor by floor, from cellar to roof.

"They've got me confused with a night watchman . . ." my mother grumbled.

As for tips, they were a lot more meager than in years gone by.

By the end of July we were the only people left in the building, apart from the Biondo's, who hadn't traveled for years because of her illness. Poor woman! So she might enjoy at least a little bit of summer, her husband would move her to the balcony after lunch, leaving her there for hours, propped up by mounds of cushions and sheltered from the sun by a straw hat with a brim as wide as a beach umbrella. I could see her from the courtyard through the foliage of the plane tree. More than once, even if I knew that paralysis prevented her from moving, I had the distinct sensation that she was wiggling her numb hand toward me in a vague signal of warning.

My father continued to go to the factory. He preferred to be a scab rather than deal with my mother's moods.

"Can you feel the peace and quiet? This is better than the Riviera," she would say. "I don't envy the folks who are going away—no, not at all. What kind of a vacation is that, with all the noise and traffic?

Everyone in cars like idiots! Beaches so crowded you can't even walk
... Now this is what I call a vacation. No one around, no more 'yes
signora, of course signora, right away, signora ... Feel how peaceful
it is! Smell the fragrance!"

In the morning and afternoon we would sit on the shaded steps,
spending long hours—she observing, me reading. When it got too
muggy we would stay inside. I would've been happy reading under
the plane tree but she always wanted me by her side, using the same
old excuse that it was too hot outside. "With this heat," she would
say, "the crazies sprout like mushrooms. It would be better not to
be outside by yourself in the courtyard ... With all the awful things
we hear on the television ... you don't want to wind up like Paul
Getty, do you?"

Inside or out, it was all the same to me. I read all day, without
stopping. I even forgot to breathe, and when my eyes were too tired I
would imagine what would happen in another month: I would soon
be starting the Classical Lyceum, where I'd meet new people, learn
ancient Greek, go downtown every day ...

On the eve of the Feast of the Assumption, the Professor moved to
Via Icaro. Unlike his mother, he brought a lot of stuff with him.
Out of the moving van came an avalanche of boxes and suitcases of
every size. The movers were two black men who spoke with him in
English. My mother was mesmerized by them. She had only ever
seen dark-skinned people on television.

"I barely noticed the move," she started to tell my father at supper.
"Every time someone else moved I had to clean for days and days after, fixing tears in the runners, rubbing out scratches on the walls and
in the elevator, skid marks on the floor ... Do you remember Signor
Puxeddu, Paride? What a mess! He was moving back to Sardinia
because Milan made him sick to his stomach. You were still little,

Chino ... Well, the morning that he finally moved out—I still hadn't opened the loge—he left this huge turd in the middle of the lobby! I slipped on it and almost killed myself! ... But those two negroes swept everything up, dusted the walls, and wiped them down. They could teach the people who live here a thing or two about manners! And they weren't bad-looking! On the contrary. Two handsome young men—tall, well-built. And the arms on them! ..."

"Negroes are big down there, too ..." my father muttered under his breath.

She continued to extol the polite manners of the Professor and his movers. She talked and talked more than she had in months.

"You can hear the water fountain ..."

"Yes ..."

"And the streetcar, too ... Listen, Professor Foschi. It's so peaceful! Another coffee?"

"No thank you."

"It seems ridiculous to keep the loge open in this wasteland ... What's the difference between a weekday like today and a holiday like the Feast of the Assumption? ... None! But the rules say that the loge can only be closed on the fifteenth—fine, keep it open, for heaven's sake. The burglars won't even have to trouble themselves by sneaking over the gate and climbing up to the balconies by the trash chute ... Free entry!"

"So you should close, Signora Elvira ..."

She placed her hand over her mouth, as if she had just heard a dirty word.

"Close! ..."

"Who'd stop you from doing it? Besides you and your family I'm the only one here ... Right?"

"The Biondos are also here, on the fourth floor. She's been paralyzed for years. At some point she came down with a strange illness, I don't know what it was ... a rare disease ..."

The Professor lowered his gaze. He wasn't interested in gossip.

"So call Signor Biondo and ask him if he would mind if the loge was closed for a few days."

"Basically it's about security."

"Security?"

"Yes, of course. There've been a few burglaries here. They wanted to break into the loge one night. What a scare! And they almost succeeded. But my husband chased them away. Every now and then he rises to the occasion ... And the burglars had already robbed two apartments at 18 Via Icaro."

"I never lock my door ..."

"Not even at night?"

"No, not even at night. If someone has evil intentions, one way or another they'll find a way in. Someone who wants to ransack your apartment is obviously not going to check whether your doors are locked. So there's no difference between a closed and an open door. The difference lies in the intentions of the person outside. And what can we do about the intentions of other people?"

His argument was too subtle for my mother.

"So, with your authorization, I'm going to call Signor Biondo and tell him that I'm thinking of closing."

"With my *authorization*?"

"Yes. Did I say something wrong?"

"Well. You did get one thing right. I have no authority ..."

"Yes, you do, you represent the condominium."

The Professor's face darkened. "Signora, who do you think I am?"

My mother didn't know where to turn. She took a deep breath and forced herself to remain calm. "Alright. Please, not another word. It would be much easier to stay open."

"Signora," he pressed on, determined to be completely clear. "I don't represent *anyone*. I can barely represent myself. And that word, 'condominium,' please stop using it, at least with me. It makes my skin crawl ... The last thing I wanted to say is that you don't need my permission. Go ahead, take the day off, leave ..."

The last part of the speech almost sounded sweet.

"If it were up to me, I'd already be an *apartment owner*," my mother said, slightly reassured. "Be that as it may, if you don't mind, I've never found the word so awful. There are words that are worse. 'Doorwoman,' for instance. Do you think it's been nice for me all these years to hear myself called a *doorwoman*? People can't say that word without adding a little venom. I wish they'd call me an apartment owner ... Did you know that before your arrival I was about to buy myself a home? I really wanted to leave, you can't imagine how badly. But in a family, in the end, it's the husband who decides."

"I'm sorry," the Professor said.

That was all. He didn't ask a single question. The private affairs of other people made him feel uncomfortable.

"You keep telling me to leave ..." my mother resumed, forcing herself to sound cheerful and friendly, "but why aren't you going anywhere?"

"I have to work. I have to finish something that I've been dragging out for a long time. Otherwise, of course I'd go away."

"Go where? I wouldn't know how to choose ... Italy is so big! To think that going from my hometown to Milan takes eleven hours on the train! And it takes just as long to go back ... Then there's Sicily, Sardinia ... But I'm not interested in vacations or trips. All I ever wanted to do was retire to my own home, close the door, and not see anyone. Like now ..."

She had suddenly become more beautiful, the way she used to be. Even my father noticed. I hadn't heard their mattress springs squeak that way in months.

Click click click click click ... *Click click click click click* ... Hunt and peck ... *Click click click click click click* ... *Ding!* ... *Click click click click click* ... The letters fell on the sheet of paper like drops of rain, the page wrote itself. *Ding!* ... *Ding!* ... *Ding!* ...

I decided to knock. The sound of the typewriter came to a stop.

"Come in ..." said the youthful voice of the Professor.

I turned the knob and pushed the door open.

"My mother would like to invite you to lunch," I said from the doorway.

From where I stood, the interior seemed to have changed. The Professor was seated at a desk that hadn't been there before and a new light, the light of summer, shone on every surface.

He stood up from the desk and came toward me.

"How kind of you. I'm happy to accept ..."

In the elevator he kept looking at me, but he didn't say a word.

My mother, certain that the Professor would accept the invitation, had already set the table for three. She had taken out the blue linen tablecloth and the tall glasses. Her lips were red with lipstick.

"Professor Foschi! Welcome! Do come in!"

"Would you please stop calling me Professor! My name is Ippolito ..."

She poured him a glass of wine.

"But I thought you were one. With those boxes and boxes of books you brought! Well, I hardly know what to call you ... if I can't call you a 'co-owner,' or a 'professor.'"

"Actually I did teach, once upon a time ..." he admitted, with a bashful smile. "Where should I sit?"

"Wherever you like ... there, in my husband's place. And what did you teach?"

"A little bit of everything, but mostly English."

"Just like the Maestra ...so, you are a Professor! Why deny it? You're always denying the obvious. You're the owner of an apartment and you say you're not an owner. You taught and you say you're not a professor. Make people respect you, you've got every right! Others wouldn't think twice about flaunting their titles, with 'contractor' or 'accountant' engraved on their name plates ..."

She was referring to Caselli and Dell'Uomo. The Professor nodded.

"They can write whatever they want on their name plates, if that's what matters to them. I don't care about titles. I think they're a form of insecurity. Even at school, when I used to teach, the kids would call me by my name, Ippolito ..."

"But that's not right," my mother protested, while piling his plate high with rice salad. "You need some distance. Otherwise the kids take advantage and lose respect ..."

"That's not true. My kids always respected me. Respect is a question of feeling, not of titles ... What difference does a title make if we don't associate it with what our feelings dictate to us? Otherwise it's just a sound, a lie ... I don't need lies. We already hear enough of them from politicians, don't you think?"

Lies! Lies! Lies! as the Maestra used to say.

"Can we please not talk about politics? I already hear enough about it from my husband! In my opinion, you, Ippolito, think people are better than they actually are. You don't know how awful they can be, from the moment they're born. They tease you, disobey you, treat you like a servant ... Listen to me, I know a thing or two about it. People are cruel!"

"You're exaggerating! ... sometimes they're cruel, but only sometimes ... Children know right from wrong—if we're honest with them. If they don't learn from their parents, they can learn somewhere else ... At school, on the street, from anyone. We can't give up hope ..."

My mother placed a hand on his shoulder.

"Ippolito, you're talking like a priest!"

He fidgeted in his chair. "You really need to label me, don't you? And now you're calling me a priest?"

"You're not offended, I hope?"

"A little," he said, ironically. "I have a hard time putting up with priests ..."

"So I was wrong to think you were a good person ... you're better off the way you are! Every good deed is punished. Take me, for example."

"Are you a good person?" he asked.

My mother was speechless. How dare he! Of course she was good! Wasn't she feeding him? If she hadn't been good, would she have spent the whole morning slicing hot dogs, opening cans of peas, and boiling rice? Couldn't the professor see for himself?

"I think I am," she replied. "I don't hurt anyone. I'm good. Absolutely. And others take advantage of me ..."

"What others?"

"What do you mean 'What others'? The tenants, the folks who have turned into co-owners. They think I'm their servant ..."

"And who lets them think that?"

"Don't look at me!"

"Are you sure you're not imagining things? That it's not one of your fears?"

My mother was starting to fret. So was I. The Professor was enjoying twisting things around too much.

"Why should I be afraid? And of what? I'm not ashamed of who I am!"

"You're confusing things. Fear is one thing. Shame is another. So let's settle this by saying you're a very proud woman ..."

I recognized the Maestra in his love of making distinctions. It was an annoying argument, but I liked it.

"Yes, you're right. I am *proud*," she conceded.

Thanks to that adjective, which sounded almost like a compliment, her good mood was restored. To celebrate she poured a little red wine into her own glass.

"Why isn't Chino at the seaside like all the other children his age?" the Professor asked, suddenly shifting the conversation to me.

"Where would I send him? I don't have any family."

"There are summer camps."

"Please. The camps are for poor children whose mothers don't want them around. Or for the handicapped kids from the asylum! Luckily my son is healthy and intelligent. And I enjoy having him home with me. We get along great, don't we? ... Luca is used to staying in Milan. He keeps his mother company. By the way, his name isn't Chino. His real name is Luca. That's what the Maestra always called him. So it's about time that the rest of us called him Luca, too. By now he's almost a man ..."

"Would you mind telling me who this Maestra is?"

"Your mother—Miss Lynd!"

The Professor turned his head toward me, giving me a severe look.

"Did you know the ... Maestra?"

"Did he ever!" my mother responded for me. "He went upstairs to see her every afternoon. If I'd let him, he would've stayed there overnight!"

"She taught me English," I explained.

"Do you know English?!"

"So-so . . ."

"Don't be so modest! Tell the Professor how many words you know! He was so crazy about English! Day and night with his notebook open. Sometimes he'd even start speaking English with me, didn't you, Chino? Do you remember?"

"How many words do you know?" the Professor asked me.

"Five thousand," I said.

He swallowed his last gulp of wine. "Then you're just the person I need, Luca."

I helped with the unpacking this time, too. I took out lamps, musical scores, fans, pitchers, cups, clocks, dozens and dozens of useless, bizarre objects that spoke of distant places and times, of long-gone days and occupations. And papers! A sheet of paper here, a card there, a little notebook. Those big boxes contained the last splinters of the glorious wreck!

How often I'd imagined what the Maestra's dictionary might look like. Here was imagination transformed into reality, the coveted second chance ... No, it was not lost, as she had wanted me to believe and—who knows!—maybe she herself believed. Her son had taken the trouble to rescue it! And I, by some twist of fortune—if my name really meant what the Maestra had wanted it to mean—found myself helping him in the final phase of the rescue.

I shook with emotion: that fundamental part of the Maestra had arrived, through countless roads, all the way here, to the sadness of Via Icaro, where I lived, and now, finally, at the end of its adventure, it was revealed to me.

Ippolito couldn't imagine how happy I was, and I didn't feel right in telling him about it. I pretended not to know the meaning of those yellowed pieces of paper, whose story, for that matter, he hadn't even bothered to explain to me. In that final phase of his venture, I was a simple assistant, an extra: the triumph belonged to him, and to him alone, the true son ...

Sitting in his living room, near the window, I started dictating. The definitions were written very clearly. Most of them were the work of copyists, but many had been written by the Maestra herself.

Through my lips passed, one syllable at a time, some of the definitions that my second mother had conceived in a long-forgotten time, when she was in love with humankind and still fooled herself into thinking she could help humanity grow through certain definitions ...

Some of the most beautiful lines from English and American literature passed through my hands: descriptions, portraits of real or imagined people, thoughts, examples ... Every page was struck through with lines of various lengths, crossing out entire passages. Because of space limitations, the dictionary required short citations, only a few crumbs of the best bread of writers, as if literature was forbidden from entering into the world of everyday language, and could only glimpse it through the bars of a deletion.

I enunciated out loud, like a teacher to a pupil, and the fun of dictating brought forth a pride that I had never felt, not even when the Maestra had paid me her first compliments. But there was a huge difference between the Maestra and Ippolito: she treated me like a child, he like a man. A compliment from the Maestra was an award; the trust of Ippolito a recognition.

We would work all morning, and at one o'clock go downstairs for lunch. Unlike the Maestra, Ippolito ate heartily. He never refused a second helping. During lunch he liked asking my mother about her work, her interests, her opinions. And although the Professor never eased up his argumentative or teasing tone, she would answer cheerfully. Someone was finally taking her seriously and listening to her.

She was curious about his life, too, and she, too, had a lot of questions for him, but the Professor had an exceptional talent for always changing the subject to something else. He didn't enjoy talking about himself, just like the Maestra. My mother tried anyway. We learned that he had stopped teaching a few years earlier, choosing to retire early so he could dedicate himself wholly to the dictionary. We also learned that he was fifty years old ... My mother was amazed he was already so *old*—the exact word she used—and she immediately tried to make amends, saying that he still looked like a youth: he had all his hair, no signs of a belly, he moved with agility, dressed like a boy. She added that age didn't matter—and, in fact, her husband was much older than her, too. Finally, after many questions that skirted the subject, she managed to ask him the one closest to her heart: "Ippolito, were you ever married?"

He didn't answer. Without explanation, he dropped onto his plate the slice of watermelon into which he had been biting—leaving a pattern in the rind not unlike the decorative motif of a wood inlay—and stood up from the table. My mother felt awful. She stood up, too.

"Where are you going? ... Don't you want a coffee?" she proposed, in an attempt to salvage the situation.

"No thank you. It's time for me to get back to my Olivetti typewriter. *Mille grazie*, I'll return the favor ..."

My mother came to the conclusion that the Professor had gotten burned when he was young. He was too good—women weren't interested in men like him, so considerate and understanding ... And they didn't deserve him! With women, especially certain kinds of women, you need to take the upper hand ... Women are witches!

She'd finally stopped acting like her life was over. The Vignolas' apartment, the building, her husband—all was forgotten. With just a touch of make-up, she hid the last vestiges of disappointment, highlighting her charming and open facial features, and kept her hair gathered in a bun, exposing her pretty neck to the light of day. Rather than her usual faded cotton T-shirt, she put on a colorful sleeveless top that emphasized her breasts and hips, and on her finger she wore her diamond. I became aware of her beauty and even found myself worrying about her, as if she were a delicate flower that would fall apart at the first breeze.

Nor did my mother's sudden transformation escape the notice of Ippolito. He noticed her diamond, too. How could he not, when she was always waving it under his nose?

"I hope you don't think that it's fake?" she teased.

"Of course I don't. You're so mean! Is it a present from your husband?"

"It's a gift I made to *myself*! I'm still paying for it ... My husband doesn't appreciate certain things. In the evening, before he comes home, I have to take it off and hide it in the closet. Otherwise all hell will break loose."

"You're kidding ..."

"That's the way husbands are. What can we do? Paride has no love for the things I care about. In his opinion I just want to imitate the signore. I know, I'm not a signora. I'm a working woman. But why shouldn't I have a ring, too? I work hard morning, noon, and night, I keep my household running—why, I keep a whole five-story building running! I don't even go on vacation! I have the right to indulge myself every now and then, don't I? But you understand certain things. I've never had anything. Look how shiny it is! Do you like it?"

"Very much ... of course ... you did the right thing, Elvira."

Two seconds later he burst out laughing.

"What is it?" my mother asked, dismayed. "Don't you like my ring? Were you lying to me just now?"

Ippolito shook his head. "No, it has nothing to do with the ring." And he kept laughing. He couldn't stop.

"So what is it, then? Why won't you tell me? Now you're starting to make me angry ..."

He held his stomach, as if he were losing his mind. "I'm sorry, Elvira, I'm so sorry." he said, when he finally calmed down. "Do you want to know why I was laughing? Do you really want to know? But you have to promise you won't get upset, because you're so touchy! I was laughing because you have the whole world."

My mother glowered. "And you think it's funny?"

"Very," he reiterated, breaking into new fits of laughter. "I'm sorry, I'm sorry ..."

"If you want me to forgive you, you'll have to accompany me to the market ... This time of year they sell tomatoes for nothing ... We can buy a whole lot and I'll prepare enough sauce to last us all winter ... And if you promise to stop teasing me, I'll give a few jars to you, too ..."

For two days crates of tomatoes were boiling in every pot and pan in the house. My mother puréed them and, after the sauce started to cool down, poured them into glass bottles she had saved. In the

bathroom one of them exploded because of fermentation and im-
printed a blood-red stain on the wall next to the mirror. Not even
soap could wash it away.

The warm scent of the sauce saturated our two tiny rooms, stuck
to our skins, and wafted throughout the building, making it all the
way to the nostrils of Signor Biondo—and poor paralytic's.

"Mmmm, it smells so good!" my mother said.

A second before getting up from the table, the Professor took a small oblong packet from the back pocket of his jeans, and with a sly smile he pushed it toward her.

"What is it?"

"A little something for you ... Go on, see if you like it."

My mother tore open the tissue paper.

"But what is it?"

"Open it!"

She opened the velvet box and let out a cry.

"It belonged to my grandmother," Ippolito explained.

"Your grandmother? No, I couldn't possibly accept it ... Thank you so much but ... I swear to God ... Thank you so much, but I couldn't ... A necklace like this is worth a lot of money. It's a family heirloom and family heirlooms are supposed to go to your fiancée. What's this got to do with me? What did I do to deserve such a gift?"

"Do you always have to do something to receive a gift? Put it on, otherwise the necklace will remain in the drawer for another hundred years."

My mother hesitated. First she wanted to make sure she really was the intended recipient: "You could always give it to some lovely lady ..."

"What do you think I'm doing now? Am I not giving it to a lovely lady?"

"Stop making fun of me! I can never be sure whether you're telling the truth!"

She pretended to make a joke of it, but she was filled with emotion. Her hands were shaking so badly that I had to help her with the clasp.

"I always tell the truth."

She didn't notice his peremptory tone.

"What would the Maestra say if she knew that the family jewels would end up around the neck of someone like me, a ... *doorwoman?*"

Ippolito furrowed his brow. He didn't like the conversation shifting to his mother. My mother tried to remedy the situation.

"Your shirt is missing a button ..."

He shrugged his shoulders. "I know. I'm always telling myself that I should fix it and then I forget."

"I'll sew it back on. Bring it to me tomorrow and we'll also touch it up with the iron. I bet you never iron."

"And why should I? I don't see the point of it. All you have to do is hang your clothes up right. It's almost the same as ironing—and that way you don't waste time or energy."

"Just like the Maestra," I thought to myself.

My mother thought the same thing, but out loud. Once again Ippolito stood up suddenly and left.

"He's really fond of you," my mother said while she was washing the dishes. "It's understandable ... A shame that he doesn't have any children. Who knows how much he misses having a family. At least I have you. But who does he have? ... That man has never received any love, not even from his mother. Life is so unfair! It's so sad! Would you have liked to have a father like Ippolito?"

I didn't answer, because the answer was yes. Realizing she'd asked a question that was too bold, that could get us both in trouble, she quickly retracted it: "I was only joking, don't misunderstand me! What's done is done, we can't change the past. Besides, where do you think we could have met, Ippolito and me? Maybe on the train or in a pastry shop, if it was our destiny." Wiping her hand over her reddened eyes she expelled the daydreams. "I can't believe the stupid ideas I come up with sometimes! As if Ippolito would go out with someone like me! Such an educated man . . . a genius!"

She struggled to dismiss a feeling that she had neither the courage nor the ability to call by its true name. That feeling would never last anyway, so why give it a name? Why let it grow? Just to kill it when it got bigger?

We were walking by the church. The sun had already descended behind low clouds, but the air was still warm, spreading a golden halo over the deserted neighborhood. In the glare of the last beams of light, the glass on the telephone booth shimmered like a mirror.

"Do you go to mass?" Ippolito asked me.

I replied without hesitating: "I don't believe in God."

He stopped walking, shocked. "You don't believe in God? . . . Everyone believes in God at your age! What made you stop believing? Something must have made you change your mind! *Or someone!* No one stops believing in God like that, from one minute to the next."

It hadn't taken him long to realize that my proud atheism—I myself was only becoming aware of it in that moment—was a product of his mother's lessons. He would have liked to hear me talk about her, but he was afraid to ask. He tiptoed around the question, testing me, testing the ground with shy allusions and indirect encouragement. I was no different. We were implicitly prohibited from comparing our memories, of composing them into a single image. Maybe we were afraid of disappointment or becoming jealous or even simply of not being able to tell the truth. She had become ineffable to us, although every day we celebrated her through our devoted commitment to complete her work.

"Let's go through the fields," I proposed, out of fear that our afternoon walk would end earlier than usual. In the underbrush, Ippolito was able to identify and name herbs and flowers, which he gathered into bouquets for my mother. He wandered, losing track of time. As we walked along the ditch he recited from memory the passage about

Renzo's vineyard in Manzoni and the diseased garden in Leopardi—
the Maestra's favorite passages!

We climbed over the low gate that separated the city from the
countryside and started to make our way through the dusty fields.
The sunset inspired him to recite French poetry. When he finished
he gave me an amused look: "Do you know who that was? Charles
Baudelaire."

We were approaching the rubble heap, a pile of crumbled cinder-
block and crooked pipes, when I saw my father. He was helping a
woman up from the ground about twenty yards from us. Ippolito
took me by the shoulders, turned me away from my father and said,
"Come on, let's go."

Through the corner of my eye I recognized Gemma, who was
dusting off her skirt. Without speaking, we retraced our steps.
We climbed back over the gate, walked past the church again, and
reached the home for the severely disabled. "I want to introduce you
to someone," he said, "if it's not too late."

He was looking for a way to distract me. Indeed, he was trying to
erase from my mind the scene we had just witnessed. Yes, Ippolito
was very fond of me. It hurt him to see me suffering. But was I suffering? It wasn't clear to me ... maybe not. My father's betrayal gave
my mother the freedom to love Ippolito without guilt.

At the end of the long avenue that started at the gate, we came to
a small park behind the office building. Amid the plants, in the fragrant air of the freshly-watered loam, two men in shirtsleeves were
shouting at a group of teenagers and children to line up. Some were
in wheelchairs, others were walking with crutches or standing up
with the aid of complicated steel armatures.

"Here she is!"

A tiny figure broke away from the group. She moved like a robot.
Ippolito went toward her and I followed him like a sleep-walker.

"Forgive me for not visiting sooner. I've had so much to do . . . I've brought a new friend with me. Luca, let me introduce you to Tilit."

This creature, of indeterminate sex, dark-skinned, where there was indeed skin, extended her slender hand to me and smiled through half a mouth. The other half had disappeared. It had been replaced with a repellant bright pink plastic mouth. Her left arm and leg had also been completely destroyed.

"Hello," Tilit greeted me, "What's your name?" Her voice emerged limpidly.

"Luca," I heard myself reply.

Tilit told me that she was sixteen years old—but her body, in the parts that had developed naturally, was that of a ten-year-old girl. Abandoned by her mother in the forest, she had been attacked by a wild animal and reduced to this, a scrap of chewed-up flesh.

"Tilit!" called one of the men in white shirts, while waving to Ippolito with one hand. "Come on, it's suppertime!"

"Can I give you a kiss?" she asked.

Ippolito gave me a look that meant, "Get closer to her." I brought my cheek close to what remained of her lips and absorbed its warmth. Ippolito leaned in, giving her a gentle hug, and said, "Enjoy your meal!"

"Come back soon!"

She took a step backward and, leaping from one foot to the other, as if she were walking on stilts, she reached the group with the dry sound of scrap iron.

I was leaving Milan for the first time.

To justify our trip, Ippolito said we'd been working too much recently. He didn't want to overdo it—every now and then the mind needs a break.

He was careful not to allude to the scene by the pile of rubble. It would've made no sense, considering the effort he was putting into erasing it from my memory.

He drove very slowly. Cars, he said, should be at the service of men—not the other way around—and if it had been up to him, we would have gone by bicycle. On the bicycle, a splendid invention, you could go anywhere. He had traveled half the world on two wheels, and had only gotten his driver's license ten years ago, at the insistence of his friends. The beat-up Fiat 128 he was driving had been a gift from one of them. A car was the last thing he wanted, but at this point he was starting to get used to it.

"I'm getting older, Luca ..."

After an hour of driving he parked next to a country church. From there we walked along a steep and rocky path, winding through the woods down to a riverbed. He was almost running, happier than I'd ever seen him, perfectly at ease.

After walking for half an hour, we rolled out our towels on a rocky beach, between the trees, deep in the gorge. "Isn't this splendid?" he repeated, "and we're only a few miles from the city!"

At first the area seemed deserted. But then, immersed in the green, I was able to make out quite a few other people. All men. All naked. Ippolito got undressed, too. He saw a couple of guys he knew and started up a conversation with them. You could tell he was a regular, like the others. I kept my shorts on.

I'd been so happy when he proposed that day of vacation, but now all I wanted to do was escape! We ate sandwiches that my mother had prepared and fell asleep in the shade.

When I woke up, he was gone. He came back a little while later, covered with sweat and dust. I took out my Latin book and tried to read a few lines. "What are you doing?" he teased. "Put down your books! Here, you need to take a nice dip in the cool water. Come on! We'll go for a swim in the Adda, the 'River of Providence.'"

I stood up reluctantly and followed him down to the riverbanks. The water swirled and foamed, even where it was shallow. Reciting a passage from *The Betrothed*, he climbed up a tall boulder and, ignoring the menacing look of the surface of the water, dove in. He reemerged a few feet away, where the water was churning with foam. He went under again. I happened to notice a sign: "DANGER: No Swimming Allowed." I raced along the bank as far as I could, following the path of the river. I wanted to shout his name, but when I opened my mouth only the faintest sound came out, covered by the roar of the current. I couldn't hear my own voice. In the distance, I saw Ippolito's head come back to the surface, and then disappear for good.

I stood there staring at the water.

When the sun descended behind the rock wall, I reached the spot where we had left our things. An older man getting ready to leave noticed that I was alone and asked the others for help. Some of the young men who'd been chatting with Ippolito offered to climb up the ridge, and from up there, try to see what had happened to *my father*. The man and I went back to where we had parked the car and waited.

The sun was setting up there, as well. When the young men came back they had no news. There was nothing left to do except report his disappearance to the local police office. One of them accompanied me there and left me at the entrance.

To simplify matters I told them I had lost my father, as the others had said. A policeman brought me home. My parents were waiting for me in front of the gate like two tormented souls. It was late at night.

The policeman questioned my parents and made them show their identity cards—he didn't believe dad was my real father until I admitted that I had lied. Once the policeman was finally convinced that Ippolito wasn't my real father, he pelted my parents with insults: the beach where Ippolito Fochi had taken me was a shameful place!

As soon as the policeman left, my father went wild. He yelled at my mother, accusing her of delivering me to a pederast—it was a miracle that I hadn't drowned. From now on I could only go out with his permission . . . Stunned by the tragedy, she said nothing and didn't move. She hugged Ippolito's clothes to her chest while tears streamed down her face and neck.

The next morning a taxi stopped in front of the gate. He wasn't dead after all! He was covered with scratches and insect bites, but he was in one piece. The merciless current had dragged him along the rocky bottom, tossing him against the sharp cliffs until, when despair had almost got the better of him, he came back up, far, far away. Struggling, very slowly, also because he was exhausted from holding his breath underwater, he climbed up a steep bank and found shelter in the woods, where he spent the night, like Renzo in *The Betrothed*. In the morning, at dawn, cutting his feet on the harsh terrain, he made his way back to the beach, where someone came to his aid.

My mother was also resuscitated. She could barely keep herself from throwing her arms around him, but, mentally, she covered him with kisses and loving caresses that healed each wound. She washed his clothes, over which she had cried all night, and hung them out to dry in the sun. That evening she took her finest skein of wool out of the basket and started to knit a sweater for him. It was time to start thinking about winter.

V

H ere I am!" she announced, drumming her fingernails against the window. A second later Signorina Terzoli opened the door and came in. "Ah, I didn't realize you had company," she exclaimed upon seeing Ippolito.

He continued eating his spaghetti.

"Signorina Terzoli, do you remember Professor Foschi?" my mother asked her coldly.

"Of course I do! Maybe he doesn't remember me, but I remember him. Wilma Terzoli—pleased to meet you."

Ippolito stopped chewing and stood up as a sign of respect, but she forced him to sit back down with a friendly pat on the back.

"Don't mind me, please, continue with your meal! My goodness, what are those scratches on your face? . . . You should put some lotion on those . . . Are you visiting?"

"No," my mother answered for him, "the Professor moved here right before the August holidays."

"Who knows why I thought he would rent out his mother's apartment—it must be so full of sad memories! . . . Anyway, I won't be any bother, don't worry. Here everyone knows I'm a peace-loving person, right Elvira? Why I'm even careful about flushing the toilet after ten o'clock at night . . . Sometimes, if all I've done is pee, I avoid flushing altogether. We shouldn't waste water, you know. In Africa they really need it, poor things . . . Well, I'll let you eat in peace, don't mind me. Elvira, I'll come back later. I have so many things to tell you! You can't imagine everything that's happened to me!"

In the meantime she cast certain gazes in the direction of Ippolito, who had gone back to eating with gusto. "I'll only tell you one more little thing, then I'll go ... I spent the summer trying to get rid of a rash. Isn't that ridiculous? I call it a rash but who knows what it really was. At first I was scared to death. My neighbor at the beach knew a dermatologist in Savona. I made an appointment to see him and he gave me a lotion. It didn't do a thing. I went back to him two more times, and each time he came up with a different diagnosis. What a waste of money! In the end he had to admit that the skin is a mystery, they know very little about it. I really like how he defined it. 'The skin is a filter.' Do you want to know what brought me some relief? ... Cabbage. I read somewhere that it has therapeutic powers. Every night I applied some cabbage leaves to the infection and now, thank goodness, it's getting a little better. Is Signora Dell'Uomo back from the mountains yet?"

My mother shook her head. "You're the first one back."

"Strange, she swore she would return by the beginning of September. I'll have to ring her up later. Anyway, I'll let you eat in peace. What did you cook, Elvira? Mmmm ... What a nice ragu! Is it good, Professor? Please, don't let me keep you from eating! My refrigerator is bare. I defrosted it before I left. Let's hope I still have macaroni somewhere in the cupboard ..."

"No good home should be without pasta," my mother concluded. Terzoli took the hint and finally went on her way.

"Why didn't you ask her to join us?" Ippolito asked my mother.

"Her? You must be kidding! Did you see her? Didn't you hear how she treated you? Terzoli is vicious! Keep your distance from her! Do you know what she's going to do as soon as she gets home? She's going to pick up the phone and tell everything to Dell'Uomo. 'The doorwoman had Miss Lynd's son over for lunch!' ... You don't know how nasty those two can be. But I couldn't care less about them—forgive me for speaking this way—and she's also going to talk about how your forehead is covered with scratches, and that you gave me a pearl necklace. They'll even start saying that my diamond came from you!"

"Don't you think you're exaggerating, Elvira?"

"Not at all. There's certain things you don't know. You can't imagine how many nasty rumors are already circulating about you."

"About me?"

"Forget I said anything. I don't want to upset you."

"But I find it amusing."

"In the past few years they've made my life impossible. I couldn't even offer a coffee to a poor old lady on the third floor! It bothered the *signore*! The loge is not a café, they said. So in the end I had to tell the poor thing to stop coming downstairs—can you imagine! And you're telling me to invite Terzoli to eat with us?"

"Then maybe it would be better if I didn't come downstairs, either."

My mother blanched. "It has nothing to do with you," she hastened to make light of what she had just said, "This is my home and I can invite whoever I want."

She knew that sooner or later Ippolito would have to stop coming, but for the moment she didn't want to think about it. Raising her voice made her feel a little more courageous.

"Let them report me to the building manager. If Signora Aldrovanti even tries to complain, I'll eat her alive!" Her cheeks became as red as fire. "How could they think I'm not allowed to have guests? What's wrong with that? No one has the right to criticize me. They're all envious, that's what they are: a pack of envious old hens!"

He was distracted, uninterested. I had to repeat each word to him two or three times. He would hit the wrong keys, moaning and groaning.

"Let's drop everything. This morning I don't have the head for it. Let's go out on the balcony for a breath of fresh air."

We sat in front of the pots of geraniums, side by side, looking out over the countryside, which from up there, in the clear air, seemed boundless. The sun was out, but in my shaded corner I felt cold.

"Do we have much left to do?" I asked.

"No, not very much . . . We should be done by Christmas."

He noticed I was shivering, so he pulled the curtain to one side so I would get some sunlight.

"And after that?"

"Luca, did my mother ever speak to you about me?"

My heart skipped a beat. The silence was broken. Finally he was introducing himself as the son of Amelia Lynd! How should I answer him? How *could* I answer him? If I told the truth, I would only hurt him.

"The Maestra was very reserved," I replied. "She didn't like talking about the past."

He didn't seem to mind. Deep down it was the answer he was expecting.

"Were you fond of her?"

"Yes, very," I admitted.

"Me, too . . . But she didn't love me, otherwise she wouldn't have shut me out of her life. She could have dropped me a line, at least before she died. I looked everywhere for a letter. I found nothing . . . She didn't even have a photo of me."

I remembered the letter she had written to me, the letter I cherished, hidden in my Latin book, and for the first time I suspected that it had been addressed to someone else, to her real son. I should've run home to get it, I should've reread it there with him, but at that moment I couldn't move. I was in a state of shock. Even dead, the Maestra hadn't lost her ability to be evasive. Who had I really been to her? And who was I to Ippolito? A stand-in for both? A go-between? By what criteria, for what purpose, had she, the dictionary devotee, attributed meanings to individual human beings?

Now I could clearly see to what extent I was Ippolito and he was me. We were two words that exchanged meanings, and not because we wanted to—as we had presumed to believe—but because she had wanted it to happen that way.

But hadn't I done the same with him? Hadn't I started to love him as a surrogate?

For me the time had also come to break the silence. Liberated from the fear of hearing "no," I asked him to tell me the story of Amelia Lynd.

I took mental note of everything, careful not to interrupt him even once, and when I got home later that night, I started to write down the gist of the story in my English notebook, the right place to conserve these revelations. Who knows, maybe one day I would write a whole book about her . . .

Her father was English, her mother Italian. They met on a cruise ship while visiting Greece and Turkey. Amelia was born a few months later, in 1897, in Rome, the city of her mother, where she grew up as an only child. Her father later managed to get a transfer from the newspaper where he was working and became the Italian correspondent for many years. Amelia studied in Rome and received her degree in classics. Every now and then she would go to England, to London, to visit her father's family. They were Jewish, but her father wasn't religious. The exact opposite. To Amelia he transmitted a strong antipathy toward any form of religion. Her mother, however, was Catholic, relatively observant, but enough of a non-conformist to marry an atheist. They still had a church wedding, but without the Eucharist, out of respect for the husband.

Ippolito, her first and only child, was also born in Rome, the same year that Mussolini came to power. His father died shortly after of tuberculosis. Widowed (in reality, they had never married, but she loved calling herself a widow), she moved to England, leaving the child to be raised by his grandparents. The only time he saw his mother was when his grandfather took him to see her in London.

In the early 1930s, when he was already a teenager, she decided to bring him back with her. So he joined her in England, where he continued the education he had begun in Italy. She was absolutely opposed to her son growing up surrounded by fascists. They lived in England, and other far-away places, for long periods, during which she herself took charge of his education. They spent some time in Palestine. She was interested in living in areas where populations were being formed. Although she sympathized with the Jews, she was very critical of their territorial claims. She slowly broke away from all of her Zionist friends, leaving Ippolito and her to fend for themselves.

At one point they moved to India, where their lives were much easier. There were quite a few Englishmen who wanted to give the country back its independence. New friendships were formed. Ippolito was also better off in India than he had been in England or Palestine. He was becoming a man. He no longer depended entirely on his mother.

When the war broke out they returned to Europe, to Rome. His grandparents fell sick and died in 1940. Amelia sold the house in Rome and emigrated to America, like some of her Oxford friends. Ippolito remained in Rome, but he immediately regretted his decision not to follow her. Without his grandparents he felt like a stranger in the city. The atmosphere was awful. He enrolled at the university, in mathematics, and completed his degree quickly. Then he joined his mother in New York. She wasn't at all happy there. She hated American materialism. A true Englishwoman, she said there were no secrets in America: everything took place in the light of day—how boring.

Once the war was over, they returned to Italy. This time they found a house in Milan, on Via Manzoni. Amelia was in seventh heaven. She was in love with the country. She was in love with the city. She said that in Milan they were finally living a real life, they were lucky to be witnessing the birth of Italy, or rather of the Italians. She believed in the people—in the factory workers, the housewives, the young

people. She believed in the revival and the renewal. She even managed
not to despise the Church, which was working so hard to resurrect a
demoralized society. For a while they received visits at home from a
priest, Father Stefani, whom Ippolito greatly admired.

But Amelia's enthusiasm did not last long. As on their previous
travels, she quickly started criticizing everything and everyone. Even
the reconstruction of Italy was proving to be a disappointment. The
priests were back in charge of civic life. The Italians were losers, not
only because they had not won the war, but also because they did not
know how to become the masters of their future.

In 1952, to the great surprise of everyone who knew him, Ippolito entered the seminary. As far as his mother was concerned, he
couldn't have committed a greater error. Their relationship frayed
and all communication between them ended after he took his vows.
Every now and then he would try to contact her, but his overtures
were always rejected. He had betrayed her. She didn't forgive him
even after he left the Church, in 1962. "You're unforgivable," she
wrote. Fifteen years would go by without another word from her.
She wanted nothing more to do with him.

Once in a while she would go back to London, where she still
had a house. At one point she sold that, too, because she needed
money. She had used up most of her enormous inheritance—traveling, maintaining herself and her child, buying an endless amount of
books, paying porters and copyists, donating money to causes that
she believed in ...

Knowing that she had been reduced to almost total poverty, and
was elderly, Ippolito tried to help her. He would send her money,
which she never accepted. One evening, on his way home from the
Home for the Disabled, he saw the "For Sale" sign on the gate of Via
Icaro 15. He decided to buy the apartment where she lived, hoping
she would be grateful for this gift, hoping she would forgive him.

In the space of a week almost everyone was back: Signorina Mantegazza with her dog Bella, the Casellis, the Zarchis, the Bortolons, the Paolinis, the Dell'Uomos, the Cavallos, the Di Lorenzos, the Vezzalis, the Lojaconos, Signor Vignola (alone, because his wife and child had gone from the mountains to the seaside).

The only ones missing were the D'Antonios, who were stuck in Naples because of the cholera epidemic, which the television was going on and on about, and the Malfitanos, who for some unknown reason were still in Sicily.

Their suntans, extra weight, rest, and rediscovered contact with their places of origin had changed them. Their voices were clearer, their accents had regained their original fullness, their movements seemed more natural.

But in two or three days they were already back to the way they used to be.

My mother, who'd already seen a drastic reduction in tips from previous years, now noticed that no one had brought her back a souvenir. "It's better this way," she said, "I only put that junk on display out of kindness. You know what I'm going to do now? I'm going to throw everything out."

She didn't waste a minute. That night, we could finally unfold my bed springs without worrying that something was going to fall.

The D'Antonios and Malfitanos also returned.

Signora Vezzali explained that on the eve of their departure, the parrot, Leopoldo, had disappeared. At first Malfitano hadn't given it a second thought. Leopoldo would occasionally fly away, especially during vacations. But he would always reappear a few hours later.

They waited for him that night, the next morning, and the rest of the week. Meanwhile Malfitano had reported the disappearance up and down Selinunte. They even put up the parrot's picture all over town. The search lasted for two weeks. Not a trace of Leopoldo. There was no way it could have been an escape (Leopoldo loved his master too much), or a bird-napping: with his pecking and his deafening shrieks, Leopoldo would have made life impossible for anyone who tried to capture him. So he must have been killed. There was no other explanation. Killed and thrown away. The master's suspicions inevitably fell on the person most interested in getting rid of him: his wife. Leopoldo hated her, as we'd seen on Christmas Eve. Had she, after years of being afraid, decided to kill him, with the complicity of her relatives? But she continued to protest her innocence. Leopoldo had chosen freedom, she kept saying. He had gone to a better place, finding some pine or eucalyptus tree near the sea.

Summer was over. So was the peace and quiet, the magical enchantment, listening to the splashing of the fountain and the chirping of the birds, talking and joking freely with Ippolito, no intrusions, sitting down to tasty meals of spaghetti or rice salad—now it was all just a memory.

Lunch with Ippolito was reduced to a pathetic ritual. Every time we sat down at the table, one of the old hens would stop by with some excuse to stare at what we were eating.

My mother became grumpy, curt, irritable. On my birthday she even avoided placing the ritual gift in my hand. She could feel all the eyes in the building staring down at her and she took it out on Ippolito, as if it were his fault, as if she were expecting him to find a solution. She was itching for a fight, going on and on about how he needed a wife, someone who would take care of him, iron his shirts, cook for him, keep his house in order.

"The world is full of unmarried men—*bachelors*," he argued defensively. "Do you think they all live in squalor, on empty stomachs, in messy houses?"

"If that were the problem, all you'd need would be a cleaning lady! A house isn't just a hole you live in. Big or small it's still a hole ... A woman, in other words, is a home."

"I *have* a home."

She didn't want to hear it. "A person gets older ... you need companionship. Otherwise what kind of a life is that? Life is already hard enough. Haven't you ever been in love?"

Ippolito's jaw tightened. "Of course I have."

"And you never thought of starting a family?"

"It wasn't possible. You should've understood by now, Elvira."

But no, she hadn't understood, and if she had, it didn't matter: "I don't believe you. Anything is possible if you want it enough. Obviously you've never met the right woman. Me, when I saw my husband I fell in love right away. Right away I knew he was the one for me. We smiled at each other ... Can you imagine? We fell in love at the factory, where I was serving him soup. And you know there was no room for fooling around in the factory! We were there to work! I sweated inside my uniform. He would bring home his overalls stained with grease—you could never get rid of the stains ... But if love arrives ..."

"Well, your husband obviously liked women," Ippolito said.

It was the first time he had made explicit reference to his sexual proclivities, but not even this stopped my mother. "My husband was only interested in the movies! Starting a family was the last thing on his mind!"

"Elvira, listen to me carefully," he begged her, forcing himself to stay calm. "I don't need a wife. You're convinced that I'm unhappy because I'm not married. You're wrong. I'm happy with my life, as crazy as that might sound to you—and please, can we change the subject and not talk about this anymore?"

But she refused to budge. "What is life without love?" she insisted, as if the argumentative role that Ippolito usually played had been miraculously handed over to her.

"Nothing."

"You see? So you agree with me!"

"Of course I agree with you!"

"But you are giving up ..."

Ippolito was flabbergasted. "My life has been filled with love and still is! You have a strange idea of love, Elvira."

"Love is like a fever," she started to theorize.

"Now you're a philosopher?"

Not even his sarcasm could stop her. "Love is a fever," she repeated, convinced of her intuition.

"Then it must be wrong," Ippolito contradicted her. "Fever is a symptom of disease."

"No," she retorted, "I mean that it warms you, it changes you. Fever colors your cheeks and makes you beautiful. The few times it has come to me I've felt as if I was wearing makeup."

"But a fever doesn't last."

"You're right. Love can end, too, just like a fever, or like makeup when you wash it away. What I meant to say is that when you're in love you see everything differently. You see the other person and feel happy."

"For me love is not for a single person but for the people, for *all* the people I have around me."

"Nonsense!"

"All I do is receive and give love because I feel surrounded by others. Am I making sense?"

But she didn't want to be one of the *others*! "What about sex?"

Ippolito was caught off guard.

"Sex?" he repeated, "what does sex have to do with it?"

"It has everything to do with it! Love is sex, kisses, embraces, *tenderness*, which is so important for a woman."

"And in your opinion there is no *tenderness* in simple co-existence? In being together, close, the way we are in this building, where we all take some part in the lives of others. For me this is love, or tenderness, as you call it." And he added, in a whisper, between his teeth, "Sex is something else. You can find it wherever you want."

"You're not making any sense! You call this hell tenderness? Open your eyes, Ippolito! The others couldn't care less about you or me. That's the plain truth. *No one loves us!*"

He abandoned us. The situation we had enjoyed that summer obviously couldn't continue, but I was expecting he would at least stay friends with me, asking me to help him copy down the last definitions or simply to accompany him on his afternoon walks. But he didn't. His excuse was that now I needed to think of school. The first year of high school was very difficult. Better that I put my energy into studying.

Now I spent my afternoons trying to memorize long lists of Greek words, transcribing their meanings in a special notebook, as I had done with English. Rita called to me from the garden, but I had no wish to spend time with her. "I have a lot of studying to do for tomorrow," I told her. The compiling and memorizing of such beautiful Greek words afforded me a new pleasure, which made up in part for the loss of Ippolito and, in some ways, reconnected me to the Maestra. On my first test in Greek, a translation of a passage on the roundness of the Earth, I got a perfect grade.

For my mother, however, there were no compensations or pleasures. Not even my perfect grade cheered her up. All she said, with an uncharacteristic blandness, was: "I thought they only gave such high grades in elementary school." She had never been so depressed, not even when my father had prohibited her from buying the apartment.

Once again suffering had stripped away her beauty. She looked at least forty years old. The pearl necklace that Ippolito had given her ended up in a drawer. The diamond was returned to the back of the closet and then to the man who had sold it to her.

While grief drove her to love Ippolito more intensely, it also made her detest him. She felt rejected, and criticized herself for showing hospitality to an ingrate. At school we were assigned to read and summarize the fourth book of the *Aeneid*, and in Dido's suffering I recognized my mother's own torment, and also in her regret and passion, which had become indistinguishable from bitterness. In reality, her Aeneas was still there, on the fifth floor, intent on recreating a miniature Troy built from words. She still harbored some hopes: sooner or later he would return, sooner or later her love would be requited. It was this hope that kept her from insulting him and, who knows, from maybe committing an ill-advised act.

In her affliction, she neglected her daily chores. At the same time, she became a particularly good guard, never leaving the window. Sooner or later he would have to appear. And when he did, she behaved strangely. Walking toward him with an excess of good cheer, she asked, "How are you doing, Professor? Are you going out grocery-shopping? You should go out more often. Why do you stay at home all day? What's to stop you from going out? ... If only I had wings!"

He gave her a concerned look. "Elvira, you look tired. Be careful not to get sick. You need some rest."

And she, jokingly, "Oh, I got all the rest I needed this summer. It was nice here, wasn't it? Better than the Riviera—isn't it true we had a really nice time?"

That simple reference to the happiness she'd felt those last days of August with him alleviated her anguish, however briefly. She wanted to say so much more, but the words caught in her throat and by the time she got them out it was too late. He was already gone. *Pazienza*, she told herself. Wait till tomorrow ... Tomorrow she would speak to him a little more, tomorrow she would get him to linger a little longer.

In the lobby Terzoli and Dell'Uomo were raking him over the coals. Evidently, the fact that he'd stopped coming by to see us wasn't enough for them.

"He's so grumpy. Who does he think he is?" the spinster brayed. Dell'Uomo, not be outdone, added, "I know! He puts on so many airs!"

"When I saw him there in the loge for the first time, like I told you, he didn't even get up, the slob! And why should he? He's a 'professor'!"

"That's the way handsome men always act. And it's worse when they're also professors!"

"Have you noticed? He says hello and immediately dashes away. He never stops to say a word or two. Is he afraid we might bite?"

"He must have something to hide. Have you seen the smirk he always has on his face? It's as if he's making fun of us. No one can convince me that he's not feeling guilty about his mother's death."

And Terzoli, raising her voice, "I wonder why he never got married."

"The seamstress says he's . . ." she replied in a voice mimicking Dell'Uomo, and rather than finish her sentence, she made a limp gesture with her right hand.

Terzoli's mouth dropped open. "Good heavens! So why was he going downstairs to the loge every day?"

"For convenience. Why else? Who wouldn't want to find their lunch all ready for them on the table. Even men like that get hungry." And Dell'Uomo gave another flick of her wrist.

The Professor had turned into the building's latest scandal. Every detail of his life was cause for alarm. Why did he wear white trousers? Why didn't he iron his shirts? Couldn't his dear friend the doorwoman iron them for him? Why did he buy chicken from the supermarket and not beef? Why did he drink Barbera wine? Where did he go in the late afternoon? And those scratches, how did he really get them? And how did he get by without a job?

One night, after hearing another malicious exchange between Dell'Uomo and a couple of other women a few yards away from the window, my mother couldn't take it anymore.

"The Professor," she exploded, making her way into the lobby, "is the most noble person who has ever set foot in this building, together with his mother, poor Maestra Lynd. Remember that! There are people in here who aren't worthy to kiss the ground he walks on!"

Dell'Uomo placed a hand over her breast, as if she were having a heart attack. "My how you exaggerate, Elvira, don't you think you're a little biased? There's nothing the least bit noble about him!"

"The Professor is a saint! He'll go to Heaven, while the people I'm talking about will go straight to Hell, every last one of them. And they know who they are."

She spent the evening in self-reproach. She should have been even harder on Dell'Uomo. She had turned into a coward. Even when she knew she was right, she no longer knew how to raise her voice.

A long time went by before he returned to us. He looked so distinguished when he came in, a little thinner, with longer hair. He saw my copy of the *Aeneid* open on the table and lit up. He browsed through the first few pages, looked up at me, and, clearly articulating dactyls and spondees, recited from memory the entire scene of the shipwreck. My mother, spellbound, forgot all about the coffee on the stove as it boiled over and splattered onto the floor.

Ippolito declared that the most beautiful hexameter in all Latin poetry was in that passage: *Apparent rari nantes in gurgite vasto*—Scattered men appear, swimming in the vast swell. He repeated it various times. Did I hear the alliteration? Did I hear the rhyme? And the scene? Magnificent! But if you thought about it carefully, that scene was hardly possible. Who could have seen them, those poor floundering men? To whom might they *appear*? Certainly not to the poet, who was not present at the event. Nor to anyone else, since there were no witnesses, except maybe the shipwrecked men, who hardly had the time or the desire to contemplate their sublime desolation. What did Virgil really mean when he used the verb *apparent*? Had I thought about it? Well, they appeared to the gods, that's whom they appeared to! Whom else? The *gods* were the witnesses—*they* were watching!

"Ippolito," said my mother gravely, interrupting his improvised lesson on Latin literature and forcing herself to step down from her ecstasy. "I have to tell you something. It's important ... the other tenants have taken a dislike to you. Excuse me for speaking so frankly, but this is no time for joking around. I told you they were horrible people."

Ippolito shrugged his shoulders. "What do you mean they've taken a *dislike* to me?"

"They think you're strange."

"Maybe I am."

My mother started to get worked up. "Come now, please try to understand. Don't be so hard-headed! For once you need to take me seriously. Nasty rumors are circulating about you." She hesitated for a moment. "They think you're *conceited, arrogant.*"

"Maybe I've become that way lately ..."

"They hate you!"

"Not everyone is capable of love."

"Ippolito, I'm not joking! These people can't stand you!"

"Why not?"

"Why not? Because that's the way they are. There's no rhyme or reason. You live alone, and no one knows what you do for a living or how you pay the bills. You're an oddball to them. There are only families here: the husbands work, the wives take care of the house, and the children go to school."

"But there are a few spinsters here, too."

"No one is worried about the spinsters, my dear Professor! At most, people feel sorry for them, because no one wants them. But a man, that's another question ... For the other tenants you're a *mystery*. Can you get that into your head? They don't know you, and since you're always in your own world, inside your own house, they all come up with the wildest ideas. That's the way people are. We all have people who dislike us. We have to be on our guard. Otherwise people will destroy us!"

"I would never have imagined my life could be the subject of so much interest. Besides, every person is a mystery, to himself and to others."

"These monsters don't care about your reasons! A word to the wise: if you don't get them to stop immediately, they won't give you a moment's peace. Do something, please. That way they'll stop talking about you."

"Elvira, you underestimate me," Ippolito observed with a hint of resentment. "Do you really think they can take away my *peace and quiet* so easily? I can't believe the opinion you have of me! Do you really think I'm so weak?"

His words did little to reassure her. "Listen to me, Professor. With everything I've seen, I know what I'm talking about."

To put an end to the discussion, he finally gave in. "Alright, I'll try to do something. But what do you suggest I do, you, who are so wise?"

She was too jealous to advise him to talk with the signore of the building. "Why don't you invite Signora Dell'Uomo's husband to the stadium?" she suggested, half-heartedly.

"You've got to be kidding. And please don't tell me to invite him to lunch. I don't know how to cook."

"Well, promise me that you'll do something. Something nice, that will show everyone how good you are, how kind ... how *normal!*"

"Children! Children!" he started calling from the balcony.

Since no one paid him any mind, he called on the intercom to ask me how to get them to come upstairs. He went down to the courtyard and managed to recruit only Rita, Rosi, and the Cavallo's son, Mirko. Everyone else said no. Signora Vezzali's son, Andrea, said the Professor was a pervert.

"A what?" asked Rita, wrinkling her nose.

In the end, Andrea came along, too.

The Professor cleared his table, and in the spot where I was used to seeing his Olivetti, he had placed a layer cake. What was the cake doing there? What were the others doing there, in *my house*? What did they know about the Maestra, about the Professor, about the dictionary? And why was Mirko sitting in the Maestra's armchair? Why was that little idiot Rosi leaving dirty fingerprints where I—and I alone—had the privilege and the right to lay my hands?

"You can sit there on the ground," the Professor said to Rita, who was giggling like a ninny. "Unfortunately I don't have any more chairs. You can take turns. I've never had so many guests at once ... Well now, here we are, all settled in. I'm happy that you came. Thank you. I'm sorry if I interrupted your games, but I wanted to meet you. My name is Ippolito."

He shook everyone's hand and repeated his name. Then he cut five slices of the cake and served it. No one dared to speak. The only thing you could hear was the sound of mouths chewing.

"There's plenty more, if you like," he encouraged them. "Andrea, hand me your plate and I'll give you another helping. You, too, Mirko. Don't be shy. Tell me about your vacations."

Andrea said that he had been in Puglia, at summer camp. He said that he'd kissed three girls in one night. Mirko boasted that he'd touched his cousin's breasts.

"Enough of that!" Ippolito interrupted them. "This is getting too personal. Certain secrets shouldn't be told. Let's hear from the girls."

Rita had visited the mother of Father Aldo in the mountains. Rosi had gone to Venice. Her aunt took her to Jesolo, on the seaside, and they ate *on the beach*.

"Why aren't you married?" Andrea asked Ippolito.

"Not everyone gets married. Do you want to get married?"

Andrea made a face that meant nothing. The two girls said that they really wanted to get married.

Mirko picked the Olivetti up from the ground and started playing with it. "Leave it alone!" I shouted, as if a thief were trying to rob me. I had never had the courage to touch the Olivetti. To me it was something prohibited, inviolable. Something *divine*.

Ignoring my jealousy, Ippolito slipped a clean sheet of paper under the roller and indicated to Mirko the letters of his name. Mirko hit the keys slowly and clumsily, and then he showed everyone the word, his name, like a trophy.

Frustrated, I stuttered: "I have to go."

He didn't try to stop me.

I remained outside with my ear against the door, listening to the snickering of the two boys and the striking of keys at irregular intervals by clumsy fingers.

"This is too much!" thundered Signora Vezzali, bursting into the loge.

We looked at her in dismay.

"Didn't anyone ever teach you to knock before entering," my mother shouted at her.

"Yesterday the Professor invited my son up to his house!"

"I know. My son went, too. What of it?"

"What of it? I'm telling you it's disgraceful! As a mother I can't tolerate this. We have to step in and do something. Elvira, don't you see what happens on television?"

"I don't understand what you're so upset about. All the Professor did is offer a piece of cake to the children! First you complain that he's too aloof and now you don't like that he's being kind and hospitable. Tell me, what do you want from the poor man? He can't do anything without you criticizing him! Control yourself, please!"

"If anyone is going to give my son snacks it's me! Who does he think he is, this *Professor*?" Emphasizing the word with sarcasm, as if she were choking on saliva, she added, "The things my Andrea came back and told me! And all that talk about sex! He even told Andrea not to get married when he grows up! Don't you realize, Elvira, we have to be careful! The world is full of perverts and disgusting maniacs. They entice you with candy or cake, and then ... I don't even want to think about it! That worm! We have to stop him! Well what can you expect from someone who killed his own mother?"

Signora Vezzali stood there in the loge spouting slander, like a rabid beast. Once she got it off her chest, she went back into the elevator.

We sat there waiting. We were expecting a call on the intercom or a visit from the seamstress, who never failed to appear when she heard screaming and yelling. But we didn't hear a word from anyone. A bad sign. A very bad sign. She had gotten him in trouble, and my mother was accusing herself. And now? Should she warn him or not? Maybe it would be better to leave it alone. He wouldn't believe her. Maybe Signora Vezzali was all bark and no bite. All she wanted to do was tell Elvira what a rotten mother she was. In the end, when everything was said and done, they were insults directed at her. Yes, better to forget the whole matter—in case she stirred up even more trouble ... But why oh why hadn't she bitten her tongue? Why in the world had she given him such bad advice?

"We're such idiots!" she fretted. "The other tenants don't care for the Professor? So what! ... Who cares! But no, I had to go sticking my big nose into it. Why, oh why? With all the good things I've done, with everything I keep doing for the people in this building— they haven't changed their opinion of me one bit! Now I look like a woman who can't protect her own son, who feeds him to the orca! I'm such an idiot! Why? ..."

She kept on saying that she was an idiot and asking "Why?" deep into the night.

Before we closed, Vezzali came downstairs again and delivered a sheet of paper, written in bold, uppercase letters, to be distributed to all the owners in the building. Everyone, that is, except Professor Foschi, for obvious reasons. The flier called for a co-op meeting on Friday, the day after tomorrow, at the parish hall. There was only one item on the agenda: OUR CHILDREN'S SAFETY. QUES-TIONS AND STEPS TO BE TAKEN. The doorwoman was urged to participate.

Fine, she would go to the assembly, since they had asked her, and she would give them a piece of her mind.

My father, sitting in his armchair with the newspaper, was overjoyed. Let the Professor play the professor, and the parents play the parents! ... Ignoring or perhaps oblivious to my mother's drama, he tried to explain to us the historic compromise being forged between Communists and Christian Democrats, the country's two biggest political parties.

Fewer than half of the owners showed up, but not a single one of the most vicious critics failed to appear.

"My dear fellow owners, thank you for turning out in such large numbers," began Signora Vezzali, the chair of the meeting, pretending not to notice the many empty seats, "and thank you, Signora Lojacono, for coming forward and testifying about your awful experience. On everyone's behalf I also wish to thank the doorwoman, who can illuminate certain questions ... So then, let us begin." And she started reading from a sheet of paper that Signora Dell'Uomo handed to her.

"Very troublesome things are happening in our building. Let me begin with the latest. Last Wednesday, October 10, Professor Foschi invited, into his home, some of our children, including my own, and for reasons that can hardly be considered commendable. By means of a tasty snack (a layer cake), this 'gentleman,' if he can be called that, tried to ingratiate himself with our young ones. It doesn't take a policeman to realize that this was a clear attempt at corrupting minors. Who in the world has ever seen an individual of that ilk, who barely nods when he runs into you, go to the trouble of offering a snack to strange children? This reeks to high heaven, that much is clear. I wouldn't be so concerned had I not observed in Professor Foschi such clear signs of imbalance and perversion. I'll leave aside his manners, which are so hypocritical and effeminate. I only wish to point out, as you all know, that he didn't shed a single tear at the death of his mother, that he suppressed the truth about her tragic demise, that he has never been married, that he has no job, or at least not a job he can mention. Nor does he ever receive visitors. Now isn't it odd that such a man—I can't even call him that—should invite our children into his home? And why is it that we know nothing about his private life? So much discretion can only hide a depraved and immoral existence. I would very much like to hear the opinions of those of you in attendance. The moment has come to step up. WE OWE IT TO OUR CHILDREN!"

"You said it was a layer cake?" Paolini specified.

"Yes," Vezzali confirmed, pleased with herself. "He also offered them something to drink. My son told me it was orange soda, and God only knows whether there wasn't some powder mixed in."

"You never know who you're dealing with," whispered Signora Caselli to Signora Rovigo.

"And what if Professor Foschi was only trying to do something nice?" suggested Signora Zarchi, getting up from her chair. "Why do we always have to think that bad intentions are lurking behind every kind gesture? I think you're dramatizing the whole thing. My daughter was there and she told me that the Professor is a very nice man, a good person ..."

"Your daughter's opinion doesn't count!" Terzoli jumped up. "Little children are gullible. Especially girls! That's why we're here. They wouldn't need our help if they knew how to recognize bad intentions." And she looked lovingly at the crucifix that was hanging over the door.

"Signorina Terzoli is right," Vezzali stepped in. "My son Andrea, who's a boy, understood perfectly that the Professor was setting a trap! 'Mamma,' he told me, 'if he'd tried to lay a finger on me, I would have kicked him between the legs.'"

"My Mirko stayed as close to the door as he could," Signora Cavallo reported.

"You yourselves are saying that the Professor never raised a hand to your children," Zarchi continued.

"If he'd even dared" the seamstress blurted out, "I would have carved his eyes out with my scissors!"

"And I'm telling you the Professor is an angel," Signora Zarchi concluded. "What proof do you have he was a pervert? A layer cake?"

The two men burst out laughing.

"There's nothing to laugh about! Do we want our children to come home covered with cuts and scrapes?" hollered Dell'Uomo, furious, using a possessive adjective that was completely inappropriate. "Bloodied and bruised? Having lost their innocence? Is this what we want? The same thing that happened to Riccardo last year—forgive me, Signora Lojacano—happening to our children?"

"Signora Dell'Uomo is right. We need to stop this before it's too late," said Signora Rovigo, also leaping to her feet.

"Ladies and gentlemen," intoned Signora Zarchi, indignant, "don't mind me, but I'll be leaving now. Pardon my saying so, but, honestly, I find this meeting ridiculous. Nothing but gratuitous alarmism." Without uttering another word, she walked out, leaving a cloud of rosewater perfume in her wake.

Dell'Uomo looked at the others and shrugged her shoulders. Terzoli tried to whisper something into Paolini's ear, but everyone could hear it. "Zarchi only talks that way because she's of the same ilk."

"Let's hear what the doorwoman has to say?" Vezzali proposed. "Elvira, you know the Professor well. You had lunch together in the loge every day this summer, it would seem. Your son, I have heard, spent long hours at his house . . . Doing *what* exactly?"

My mother roused herself from a kind of daze. "I know the Professor well enough to consider him a fine person," she affirmed, with one hand over her heart. "My son, it's true, spent a lot of time with him this summer, and I can assure you that nothing bad happened to him."

"Are you sure?" Vezzali insinuated.

"Of course I'm sure! My son was helping the Professor write

an English dictionary. The Professor is a lexic ... a lexic ..."—the word wouldn't come to her, and I whispered it but she didn't hear—"what I mean to say is, he writes dictionaries. You think he doesn't work, but you're wrong. He works very hard! He's always hunched over the typewriter, do you understand? Can't you hear the typing through his door? He *defines words*!"

The chairwoman wasted no time commenting on this piece of information. "And your son acted as his assistant, no less? How is it possible that a Professor comes to choose a boy as an assistant? The whole thing sounds like a setup! Don't you think that maybe the Professor took advantage of your son's innocence? We all know how certain things go: the older person wins the trust of the younger one through some kind of reward and then, when he asks for something in exchange, the younger one can't say no."

"I wouldn't even dream of it!" my mother responded. "Do you think I would leave my son in the hands of a maniac?"

"I'm not saying that you knew ..."

"I repeat: the Professor is a good, honest man. There's not many good people like him left in the world. He doesn't even see the evil around him! He would never do anything bad ... He is ... a genius! None of you understand. If he seems strange, it's because his mind is occupied with his own thoughts, with Latin, with English. He knows lots of poems by heart. All of literature ..."

"You hear what the doorwoman's got to say?" the seamstress laughed. "You can't expect her to betray her little Professor. Why don't we ask her how much money she socked away from their little lunches?"

"What? How dare you!" my mother snapped. "My money I earn myself, off the sweat of my brow."

Dell'Uomo asked her to calm down, but she could not be contained. "You invited me here to cover me with shit!"

"Nice way to express yourself," said Terzoli, scandalized.

A hubbub filled the room. No one had ever seen my mother like this, not even me.

"Silence! Silence!" Dell'Uomo repeated.

My mother looked at her, eyes ablaze. "You should all be ashamed of yourselves. You think you're so high and mighty because you bought yourselves a hole in the wall, but you're nothing but derelicts! I would never want to be like you. You're cruel! You wouldn't hesitate to lock up Jesus Christ himself. Keep away from me! You're the ones who are perverts, not people like the Professor!"

Paolini pointed her index finger at her. "Watch your mouth!"

"We're not going to let her get away with this," thundered Rovigo, "write everything down in the minutes."

My mother was beside herself. "You're nothing but a gang of bullies! Dirty liars! You should be ashamed of yourselves!"

"You sold your soul to the devil!" cried the seamstress. "You'd do anything for money!"

"You ugly cow!" my mother retorted. And she hurled herself at the woman. If Vezzali's husband hadn't stopped her, the seamstress would've lost a few teeth in the melee.

"And the rest of you have nothing to say?" my mother asked the others, who were observing passively, as if they were at the movies. "You let them insult me like that without saying a word? Cowards!"

She was right. No one said anything.

"Let's hear what the son has to say," Paolini proposed out of the blue. Those few words were enough to restore the silence.

"Good idea. Let's hear what the doorwoman's son has to say," Vezzali seconded her.

I stood up and turned in their direction. They were hideous, each of them, even the meeker ones—a rush of ill feelings had left a grotesque frown on their faces. I started to say that the Professor and I were friends, that ... my tears kept me from continuing. I still felt as if I were in his hallway, waiting for his voice to call me back ...

"You see? What did I tell you!" Vezzali exulted.

The smell of smoke forced the tenants on the fourth and fifth floors to rush out of their apartments.

Terzoli, who had more foresight than the others, brought with her a full battery of belongings. The only baggage that Signor Biondo carried was his wife, hanging onto his neck, who, in the commotion, looked like a sack of potatoes. He reminded me of Aeneas fleeing Troy with Anchises on his shoulders.

"Over there, Signor Biondo," my mother instructed him. "You can lay her on my bed."

The fire truck parked by the fountain. A team raced up the stairs with the water pump and evacuated the lower floors, where the residents continued to ignore what was happening above them. A group of men stood in the lobby to prevent more people from coming in.

My mother switched off the central electricity and went down to the cellar to turn off the gas before the whole building exploded. Flames came through the three windows in waves, sharp in the darkness of the winter afternoon. Everyone was staring at them from the center of the courtyard. Men and women, tall and short: shocked, silent, as if observing the apparition of a miraculous star. Everyone, except the Professor, who had decided not to come back home that evening.

The fire was out in a few minutes.

"Damn him, anyhow!" shouted Dell'Uomo, returning to the lobby with a gaggle of her followers. "A few more minutes and our apartments would have gone up in smoke, too!"

The sound of the firemen putting out the blaze echoed through the stairwell.

"Damn him!" repeated Terzoli. "You can smell it all the way down here. For Pete's sake! What are those guys up to now? I'm afraid they're going to break into my living room with their axes!"

And Vezzali. "He's going to have to pay for us to stay in a hotel!"

And Rovigo. "But the water damages the walls! I don't want any leak."

And Paolini. "We'll have to change everything, from top to bottom, apartments and stairs. Luckily the building's insured. By the way, Elvira, have your already notified the manager?"

And Vezzali. "But for Foschi's apartment, the condominium mustn't pay a penny! Make sure you tell Aldrovanti, Elvira. NOT A PENNY!"

They blamed the whole business on the Professor, the only one who had lost everything. No one was thinking, no one dared to talk about revenge, not even the ones who, only two days earlier, at the notorious meeting, had possessed the courage to laugh. Not even Zarchi, who certainly didn't believe the Professor was guilty of anything, much less the fire. To avoid stoking their anger, she only said that everyone would have to keep their windows open for a few days and the smell would disappear.

"Brilliant," Dell'Uomo attacked her, "all we need now is pneumonia!"

"Pneumonia would be a blessing!" her husband intervened. "All this smoke causes cancer!"

Once they had finished ranting, they went upstairs and quickly rounded up articles of clothing, and to the beat of carefully-staged coughing, migrated en masse toward the homes of friends and relatives. The only thing left in front of number 15 was our car and the car of the Professor.

The firemen finished carrying out the debris.

"You weren't able to save anything?" my mother asked the chief.

"What is it we were supposed to save, signora?" he replied ironically.

Before Christmas the tenants had another meeting. The result of the vote was announced in a letter from the manager, sent by certified mail.

> This is to inform you that the residents of Via Icaro 15, at their meeting of December 10, 1973, have decided to abolish doorman service for budgetary reasons. The rooms should be vacated by March 31, 1974. You are being offered the possibility to remain in the apartment with your family for a monthly rent of fifty thousand liras.

They were taking away both her job and her home, punishing her in the most vile manner possible. Yet she, the doorwoman, was not upset. A veil of relief had been spread over her tired soul. Finally she would be leaving that place. Finally she could turn her back on those people—it was an honor to be kicked out!

My father, instead, found the situation humiliating and dishonorable. He asked his trade union for help but, finding there was little they could do, said he was ready to pay rent. My mother, scandalized, called him crazy and threatened to ask for a divorce.

"If only you had let me buy an apartment when I wanted to," she threw in his face, although now she was glad she hadn't bought a home in that vipers' nest.

On December 24, in the late afternoon, there was a knock on the door. I was studying the subjunctive mode in ancient Greek. My mother was watching television. We weren't expecting anyone.

"Who is it?" I asked.

Silence.

"Who is it?" my mother repeated.

More silence.

She got up and peeked through the shutters.

"What are you doing there like a mummy? Come in, come in!"

He was almost unrecognizable. He had turned older, uglier—
years seemed to have passed since the fire. Even before he sat down,
she told him we were being evicted.

"How is that possible? I'm so sorry!"

"Don't be sorry, Professor! I'm happy. They wanted to punish me,
too. They never forgave me for being your friend. I'm the one who is
sorry for you—I should've opposed them more staunchly. But who
would've believed those witches could go so far?"

"Where will you live?"

"I'm sure we'll find a place somewhere. I'm not worried. I'm not
worried about anything anymore. What's the point? ... We're going
to apply for public housing, then we'll see. I've set aside some money.
Maybe one day my husband will resign himself to the idea of getting
a mortgage."

I was still angry with Ippolito. I'd forgiven him for abandoning
me—I understood that to keep his distance from my mother, he also
had to keep his distance from me—but I couldn't forgive him for the
loss of the dictionary. He was the one who was really responsible for
its destruction. The fire had been set by his blindness, by his stupid
ideals ... Since that night I hadn't been able to stop thinking of all
the words that had been lost, words that would never again return.
Never again. So much of my life had gone up in smoke along with
them. The scene was still playing out in my mind: the seamstress and
Vezzali vandalizing the apartment while Dell'Uomo stood look-out
on the landing. And the seamstress who dumped all his papers on

the ground and lit the match ... And then, in a flurry, each of them racing home.

"Listen, Elvira," the Professor resumed in a deep voice, reaching his hand out to the cup of coffee being offered to him, "I wanted to propose something ... I don't think you need to apply for public housing. Who knows how long it would take? ... Why not take my house?"

My mother gave him a severe look.

"Really. Please accept it," he insisted, "I won't be coming back here."

"What are you talking about?" she said defensively, like the time he'd given her the pearl necklace. "I couldn't possibly ... don't you realize?"

She took the sponge and wiped down the surface of the gas stove.

"I'll sell it to you!" he proposed, with a melancholic enthusiasm. "Didn't you say that you wanted to buy a house? I'll give it to you for half of what I paid. It's not a lot of money ... and with what you have left you can fix it up the way you want. There's a lot of damage."

"I couldn't. I mean it," she repeated.

"Pay me when you can! Please, say yes ..."

"You are too kind, but really, I couldn't. I can't live in a place where they did this to us. Professor, do you realize what they did to you? ... You are a true gentleman... You're a *genius*. I knew it the first time I met you—even though all of your arguments tried my patience. I told those witches, but look at how they treated you instead! You didn't deserve it—that's for sure ... And I wasn't strong enough to help you when we still had a chance ..."

Succumbing to tenderness, which restored the color in her cheeks and the spark in her eyes, she wasn't worried that my father might return or that I was there in the room, hearing and seeing everything.

"You are a true gentleman, Ippolito," she repeated, unable to find another way to express what she had been feeling in her heart for too long. "I mean it. I admire you so much, Professor ... I don't know what I wouldn't do for you ... You did notice, didn't you? Everyone else did ..."

He shook his head, disconsolate.

"Please stop, don't say that, Elvira. You need to be happy with your life, with your husband, with your son."

"You're the best man I've ever met."

"You're wrong. You don't know anything about me!"

"I'm not wrong. I know *everything* about you!"

She shivered, as if she had a fever. She took one of his hands in hers, kissed it, and in a sudden gesture wrapped an arm around his neck.

"What are you doing, Elvira?" he scolded her, trying to break her away from him. "Come now, we're not children! Stop!"

Since he couldn't pull her arms off him, he slowly and compassionately hugged her sobbing shoulders. In the sudden silence, the only thing you could hear was the electric hum of the refrigerator. I placed my hand on her shoulders, too. For a moment we became one person. For a moment the barriers that divided us disappeared. For a moment ...

My mother's tears stopped. She straightened her spine and her head. A thousand thoughts flashed through her mind and vanished into an unknown distance amid the batting of her moist eyelashes.

"Where have you decided to go?" she asked him.

"Me? ... Well, I was thinking of moving ... I'd like to go to Africa or maybe return to India. I don't know yet."

She had no comment.

They spoke to each other like two strangers.

The Professor stood up and reached for the doorknob. "Oh, I almost forgot something." He reached into the left pocket of his over-coat and took out a packet. "This is for you, Luca. Merry Christmas."

I followed him with my gaze from the bedroom window all the way to the gate. He took a few more steps and vanished into the darkness.

I withdrew into the bathroom and ripped away the newspaper pages in which it was wrapped ...

What was it? A steel comb, all black, in the shape of a shell? ... A closed fist of many fingers? ... The skeleton of a fan? ... No, it was a mechanical spider that moved its legs over my palm like a living, breathing creature ... No, it wasn't that, either. So what was it? All of a sudden I understood. The Professor had given me the heart and soul of his beloved Olivetti! Those impatient, movable legs were the typebars! The fire hadn't consumed them. It had only blackened them. You could still see the letters perfectly.